THE
WINNING
INGREDIENT

A NOVEL

THE
WINNING
INGREDIENT

A NOVEL

KELLY SWAN TAYLOR

LINK
PRESS

Published by Link Press

Providence, Rhode Island

The Winning Ingredient – First edition
Copyright © 2021 by Kelly Swan Taylor

Cover design and illustration by Michael Borkowski
Interior images by Jonathan M. Taylor

Library of Congress Control Number: 2021915821
ISBN: (hardcover) 978-1-7376244-0-0
ISBN: (ebook) 978-1-7376244-1-7

For everyday heroes:
> *From passionate small business owners*
> *—who put everything on the line for the*
> *American Dream,*
>
> *to Gold and Blue Star families*
> *—who make the ultimate sacrifice so*
> *that all of us may achieve it.*

And,

For Jonathan, my number-one fan and forever teammate in this crazy game called life.

Chapter 1

O uch! Shoot!" Mia hissed with a wince, watching the old football wobble down the rickety wooden staircase. *Bounce, bounce, bounce.* She rubbed her sore toe, silently cursing herself for her carelessness. It was hard enough maneuvering around the narrow stairwell during the day, let alone in the faint light of dawn. She held her breath and stood rigid, listening—through her pounding heart—for any movement above. Hearing only the muffled *chirps* of birds in the distance, she blew out a sigh of relief and padded down the remaining steps. She retrieved the ball, lightly brushing it off before cradling the ratty relic under her arm.

Rounding the corner, Mia pushed into the kitchen and flipped the light switch. Her mood brightened with the room, finding her own gleaming cobalt KitchenAid mixer patiently waiting for her. "Let's do this!" she whispered, rubbing her hands together. She spun the football a few times in her palm and gingerly placed it beside her book bag, then grabbed her dark blue apron from its hook.

This had become her ritual for six weeks running. Mia would wake before the break of day, sneak down to her parents' bakery kitchen, experiment, and then disappear as quickly as she came. Her mom had managed to discover her scheme but, thankfully, agreed to keep it their "little secret."

Mia peeked out the swinging door, squinting through the quiet darkness for any unexpected visitors. Feeling her chest relax, she tiptoed back to the far corner of the kitchen and climbed to the top of a step stool. With a delicate hand, she pulled out a tattered and stained recipe book from the high shelf. She ran her fingers over the worn cover, imagining her Sicilian great-great-grandmother standing beside her. Flipping halfway through the book, she whispered, "Yes! Here it is. Thanks again, Nonna." She reached into her apron pocket for her cell phone and snapped a picture of the raggedy page, then returned the book safely to the shelf.

Once again on solid ground, Mia preheated one of the ovens, giddy with excitement. As she collected her ingredients from the pantry shelves and refrigerator, she groaned when a mass of her long, unruly hair impeded her view. "Seriously? *Every* time!" Leaning into her reflection in the stainless mixing bowl, her deep blue eyes concentrated on her thick, ebony locks. She gathered them from the small of her back with a *grunt* and wrapped them in one of the ties she always kept in her apron.

"Finally!" she said, ready for the fun part. After dropping sticks of butter and scoops of sugar into the bowl, she precisely creamed the mixture to a light and fluffy texture. Continuing to add ingredients, she synchronized an online tutorial with the stained paper in the digital photo, brimming with her great-great-grandmother's flowery penmanship. All the while, she jotted down meticulous notes on her tiny, overflowing notepad.

Two large batches later, as rays of sunlight illuminated the horizon and footsteps creaked overhead, Mia placed the cooled cookies into a large plastic container—her master-piece complete. She was drying the mixer's stainless bowl when her mom popped her head into the room. "How's it going?" she whispered, her blue eyes bright.

"Awesome, Mom!" Opening the container, Mia shared one of the buttery cookies she'd concocted, eagerly lean-ing forward.

Flicking a glance toward the door, her mom's tight smile relaxed as she enjoyed a bite. "Mmm," she said, closing her eyes. "These are amazing. What are they exactly?" She inspected the details of the cookie, turning it over and over in her hand.

"I combined our butter cookie recipe with a bit of short-bread. Then, I dipped them in dark chocolate and sprinkled some sea salt on top. The trick is tempering the chocolate perfectly, so it looks shiny and not dull."

Mia's mom patted her on the back. As she peered farther into the container, she pointed to a stack of simple speck-led discs. "And what are these ones here?"

"These have rosemary in them. I used less sugar, so they're savory, like English biscuits."

Bringing a cookie up to her nose, her mom grinned as she took in the delicious pine-like fragrance. "Oh, sweetie. These are lovely." Taking a bite, her smile broadened. "You know who else would think so?"

"Our dedicated customers?" Mia squealed, her chest swelling with pride.

"Yes. And your dad. Mia, why don't you let him try one?"

Snapping the container shut, she gave her head a defiant shake. "No, Mom. You know Dad hates changes to the bak-ery. I'm not ready yet. It has to be *perfect*."

Mia's mom reluctantly nodded and was lifting the last morsel of cookie to her mouth when they heard footsteps approaching. "You'd better get cleaned up for the day," she whispered. Her eyes darted to the door as she consumed the evidence. "I need to get some things in the oven."

After sliding the cookie tub into her backpack, Mia dashed to the far corner of the kitchen, carefully returning the football to its spot on a lower shelf with an affectionate pat. She raced out the door in time to crash full-on into her dad's white chef's jacket. "Hey, kiddo! Where's the fire?" he asked with a roaring laugh.

Mia looked up at her dad's grinning face, his boisterous ebony ringlets already sticking out from every angle. "Uh, no fire, Papà. Just excited to help out in the bakery before tackling another busy day at school," she fibbed, smiling weakly at her mom behind her.

He reached down, engulfing her in a bear hug. "Yes! My straight-A student. Brand-new school year, and you're already racking up the awards." Mia immediately regretted showing her parents her recent "Algebra All-Star" award. There was no question she was proud of her grades, especially in her favorite subjects of math and science. But she knew her dad would be sharing the "news" with everyone who came in that morning for a cappuccino, biscotti, or "cannoli-to-go."

"Well, better get to those hungry customers!" she said, maneuvering around her dad.

Relief washed over her ... until he yelled back, "Hey. Hold on a sec."

Mia's stomach dropped as she turned around. Her dad slowly reached in and brushed some stray flour from her cheek. Pushing out an uncomfortable laugh, she said,

"Oops. Been helping Mom with the biscotti. I'm such a messy baker."

When he'd disappeared inside the kitchen with a nod of his head, Mia let out a shaky exhale, nearly keeling over. "That was close," she said to her mom. They'd managed to keep their secret ... for now.

Chapter 2

"M rs. Rossi! Good morning!" Mia exclaimed, straightening her apron as she stood behind the long marble counter at the back of the bakery.

The older woman with the silver bun and long trench coat beamed at her. "Morning, Mia! Shouldn't you be getting off to school by now?"

Mia upturned her wrist, checking the time. "Oh. Yeah, in a bit. Running late this morning because I had to let the chocolate set ..." She stopped herself and flashed Mrs. Rossi her biggest smile while keeping a keen eye on the kitchen door. "So, anyway, your usual?"

"Of course, my dear." Mia used her tongs to grab two almond biscotti from the glass case as Mrs. Rossi reached over to touch a strand of her shiny, dark mane. "My, my, I swear your hair grew a full inch since yesterday! How beautiful."

Mia shrugged. "It's possible. My mom doesn't want me to cut it. She must think I'm like Jo from *Little Women*, and it's my 'one beauty,'" she joked, batting her long eyelashes and dramatically flipping her ponytail.

As they both laughed, Mia's mom slid Mrs. Rossi's cappuccino across the counter. "What did I miss?"

"Uh, nothing, Mom." Mia winked at Mrs. Rossi and carried the dedicated patron's biscotti plate and porcelain cup and saucer over to her usual seat.

She had barely sat down when Mia's dad bounded out of the kitchen toward them. "Sophia! *Buon giorno!* I have some of our special cannoli ready for you to take home." He gave Mrs. Rossi a hug and a white cardboard box tied with the bakery's signature red and white string.

"Oh, no, Anthony. I really shouldn't," she said, waving it away.

Mia giggled, knowing Sophia *always* took some of their "special cannoli" home. Of course, she quickly plucked it from his hand with a wink and a *"Grazie."*

"Prego, Sophia. Did you hear about my fantastic Mia's 'Algebra All-Star' award? She's such a math whiz." Anthony's smile radiated as brightly as his chef's jacket while he gave his daughter a warm squeeze. "Mia, why don't you go upstairs and grab that wonderful certificate to show everyone?"

Mia was mid-eye roll when she heard the *jingle* of the shop bell over the bakery door. "Harper! Chloe!" she exclaimed, running to her friends. "You guys literally gave me a saved-by-the-bell moment just now."

Harper removed her bike helmet, shaking out her frizzy, short strawberry blonde hair. "Anytime, boss. You ready for school? Chilly out there."

"What masterpiece do you have for us today?" Chloe squealed, adjusting her stylish dark-rimmed glasses.

"Chloe! Incognito is not your strong suit," Harper hissed, punching her in the arm.

Mia snatched a used coffee cup from one of the tables before lifting her apron over her head. "Just give me a minute to grab my stuff."

"Well, I'm getting some biscotti while I wait," Chloe said, dashing toward the counter as Harper heaved an exasperated sigh.

Twenty minutes later, the girls pedaled through the gates of George Washington High and parked their bikes. They removed their helmets, and Mia breathed in deeply. She was greeted by the familiar scent of damp grass coming off the sprawling football field, now brimming with activity. As she scanned the stadium, labeled "Home of the Eagles," members of the varsity football team were racing up and down the lush field in their navy-blue and gold practice jerseys, engaged in an intense game of one-on-one. Mia stood mesmerized, until Chloe broke her concentration. "So? What's the theme for today?"

"Oh, right!" Mia unzipped her backpack and slid out the plastic cookie tub. "Today, ladies, is 'sweet *and* savory.'" She could practically hear the "oohs and aahs" when she popped open the container, releasing the buttery aroma.

"OMG, Mia! These. Are. Yum," Chloe said, munching enthusiastically. "They totally melt in my mouth."

Harper jerked her head in agreement. "You've done it again, boss. Zach is gonna love these rosemary ones." Mia grinned proudly, handing over the cookies.

With her friends enjoying their morning sugar rush, Mia turned her attention back to the busy football field. Strolling over to the fence lining the emerald turf, she squinted against the early-morning sun. All of a sudden, she jumped up, instinctively catching a stray ball almost before she knew what had happened. As she looked down at the football, held tightly between her palms, half the field started applauding. Mia delivered a dramatic bow, then noticed a set of sparkling hazel eyes approaching, his arms extended.

"Did you lose this?" she asked the tall, muscular boy, with wavy, dark brown hair peeking out of his gold helmet. There was no question he was attractive, even with the huge scowl he was wearing behind his facemask. When he reached out his arms yet again, Mia threw a perfect spiral directly into his hands. He gave a simple *grunt* and ran away without a word.

"You're welcome!" she yelled in a sharp tone.

Mentally shaking her head, she turned from the fence, then heard her name. Pivoting back, she spotted her best friend Zach's towering figure sprinting toward her. "Hey! Awesome catch!" He gave her a high-five and removed his helmet, damp from the morning dew. "When are you gonna join the team already?" he asked, catching his breath as he relaxed against the fence.

Mia gave a simple shrug. "Eh, no time. Plus, you guys kinda suck. No offense."

"No offense taken. 1-and-2 is *not* the right way to start the season." Zach shook his head, referring to the football team's recent losing streak.

"How'd you manage to get that one win against Pleasant Valley anyway?"

"You can thank Logan for that, with his awesome kicking. And they kinda suck, too."

Mia tapped her chin, deep in thought. "That's right. Didn't we beat them last year only because their receiver ran the wrong way into *our* end zone?"

"Yeah, sadly. But things are changing." When she gave him a blank stare, he pointed to the guy with the football and the perpetual scowl. "Now, we have a *secret weapon!*"

She squashed a grimace. But, shifting her attention back to the field, she couldn't deny what she was seeing. Whether rushing, throwing, or tackling, he looked like a future Heisman winner in the making.

Mia was about to inquire about this "secret weapon" when Chloe ran up to Zach, shoving the tub of cookies in his face. "You have *got* to try these! Mia is an absolute genius!"

Zach laughed, choosing a rosemary shortbread. "Wow, Mia! These definitely are your best. Thanks!" He scooped up a handful and rushed off with a wink. As he left Mia in his sugar dust, she stole one more glance at the football field, just in time to catch that set of hazel eyes staring back at her.

Chapter 3

When the bell rang a few minutes later, Mia was crossing the threshold of her ninth-grade honors science class. "Good morning, Ms. Marsh," she cheerfully greeted her teacher, who was poised in front of an old-fashioned chalkboard.

Smiling broadly, Ms. Marsh abandoned her metal chalk holder and waved her "star" student over to her desk. "Morning, Mia. I was wondering if you could do me a favor today."

"Of course," she said, beaming.

"I know you're usually lab partners with Chloe, but I was hoping you could help our new transfer student instead."

Mia looked over at her lab station and almost gasped. To her shock and dismay, sitting in Chloe's seat was none other than the "secret weapon" from the football field.

After her initial jolt had waned, she turned back to Ms. Marsh, forcing a smile. "Sure. No problem," she said, through gritted teeth.

Her teacher clasped her hands together in excitement. "Wonderful! Thank you." As they sauntered over to Mia's lab station, her new partner stood, surprise in his eyes. "Mia, this is Bryce Fitzgerald. He just transferred from Chadwick Academy."

Mia did a double take. "The boarding school?" she blurted out.

He gave a mere hint of a nod as Ms. Marsh continued her introductions. "This is Mia DeSalvo. She's our top student and the ninth grade's class president," she announced proudly. Mia barely waved, knowing nothing her teacher said was ever going to impress a Chadwick student.

"Pleasure to meet you," he mumbled, offering his hand.

As Mia took it, she couldn't help but notice Bryce was even better looking up close. His hazel eyes, surrounded by striking flecks of blue and green, seemed to reflect everything around him. And she swore he had dimples, if he ever managed to smile enough to show them off. His football practice gear was replaced with a more formal cashmere V-neck sweater in navy, pressed dark slacks, and matching loafers. But, despite his undeniable attractiveness, he seemed like a total bore.

Mia took her usual seat, now beside Bryce, as Ms. Marsh started the lesson on Newton's first law of motion. Shooting a look over her shoulder at Chloe behind her, she rolled her eyes at her new lab partner. Chloe almost fell off her chair, unable to hold back the giggles.

After a detailed explanation on "the concept of inertia," where Mia took meticulous notes while Bryce listlessly stared out the window, Ms. Marsh passed out worksheets for the day's experiment. Breezing over the instructions, Mia nodded. "Yeah. This seems pretty easy. Just have to get the penny in the cup, using inertia." Setting up a playing card over a plastic cup, she placed the coin on top. "You want to try first?" she asked the side of Bryce's head, pushing the cup toward him.

"What?" he asked, finally meeting her gaze.

"Do you want to try this?" she asked, enunciating her words. With barely a shrug, he lazily pulled the card from the cup, shooting the penny across the table.

Mia did another eye roll, replacing the card and coin. Quickly flicking the card as described in the instructions, the penny fell straight into the cup. "Excellent!" she exclaimed as Ms. Marsh walked by, looking pleased. Bryce shrugged again, focusing his attention back out the window.

When the bell rang, Mia was grateful for the opportunity to bolt out of the classroom and away from her snooze-worthy lab partner. "One second, please," Ms. Marsh said as Mia flew past her desk, making a beeline for the door.

Backing up, she smiled at her teacher. "Um, yes?"

Ms. Marsh offered her an envelope. "This is for your parents."

Taking the envelope, addressed, "Emery and Anthony DeSalvo," Mia started to panic. What had she'd done to solicit a personal note to her mom and dad? "Um, okay," she croaked.

Now, forgetting her hurry, she turned toward the door in a daze, but stopped when Ms. Marsh clarified, "It's also from Mr. Thompson." Mia stared at the envelope, puzzled as to why her science and math teachers had teamed up to send a note to her parents. "We were hoping you would agree to, well, tutor a student in your free time."

"Really?" Mia's eyes grew bright and wide at such an honor. "Who?"

When Ms. Marsh's gaze moved across the room toward her lab station and Bryce's lingering figure, Mia's heart sank. Her teacher studied her for a moment. "Well, give it some thought and discuss it with your parents." Although the "top student" preferred to chuck the envelope into the closest trash can, she reluctantly deposited it into her bag.

Finally, heading for the door, Mia heard the *clink* of a coin. Glancing over her shoulder, she noticed Bryce, flicking the card off the cup in perfect form as the penny fell straight below. She cracked a smile, thinking, *Well, there might be some hope for you yet.*

Chapter 4

L et me get this straight. Ms. Marsh wants you to *tutor* our new football star?" Harper asked, huddled around Mia's locker after school.

Mia sifted through her backpack with a shrug. "Yeah, I guess."

Harper looked over her shoulder, then lowered her voice to a whisper. "Word has it he used to be Wellington Prep's star quarterback through middle school. Apparently, he started Chadwick just this year."

Pausing in front of her locker, Mia drank in this new information. Chadwick Academy was located a few hours away and had a fantastic boarding school reputation. But Wellington Prep was by far the most exclusive private school in the area and known for its amazing sports teams. "Hmm. Wonder why he left Wellington for boarding school. I mean, Chadwick doesn't even have a football team." She shook off the thought, fishing inside her locker for a few books.

"Anyway, I doubt he's interested in anything I have to say. I bet he only agreed so he can get his grades up to play."

"Who cares? He's seriously cute," Chloe said, a wistful look in her eyes.

Mia grumbled, "Maybe. But he has the personality of a piece of cardboard."

"Well, if I were you, I'd try and find out why he's not at Chadwick anymore. I mean, ditching boarding school has got to be a good story," Harper added.

Mia conceded she had a good point. Why would anyone transfer after less than a month at their old school? It was intriguing.

When she got home from school, Mia didn't give the envelope another thought until she opened her backpack later that night to start her homework. As it stared back at her, sandwiched between her science and algebra text-books, she gave it her best scowl. *Well, now or never, I guess,* she thought, blowing out some exasperated air.

She found her mom holed up in their study, her eyes shifting between a handwritten ledger and the spreadsheet on her laptop. Mia watched the scene with curiosity as her mom would rub her forehead, squint her eyes, then sip from her coffee cup. Occasionally, she would sigh or groan before repeating the same process. After several minutes of this, Mia gave in and approached from the shadows. "Mom? Do you have a sec?"

"Hmm," she said, still engrossed in her screen.

"Uh, Mom? Earth to Mom?" With still no response, Mia sighed to herself and turned to walk away. It wasn't like she wanted to give her the stupid envelope anyway.

"Honey?" When Mia spun around, her mom was peering up at her through her reading glasses, the lenses magnifying the fatigue in her eyes. "I'm so sorry, hon. This stuff doesn't make any sense. I have no idea why it won't add up."

Stepping up to the papers on the desk, Mia said, "You really need to get Dad a handwriting lesson," chuckling at the barely legible pencil marks. "Mind if I have a look?"

Her mom threw up her hands and pushed back from the laptop. "Have at it. I certainly can't make heads or tails of it."

Mia hesitantly leaned into the screen and then the ledger. Her deep blue eyes narrowed to slits as she meticulously moved numbers around in her head. Suddenly, she smiled. "Of course, Mom. Look here—you forgot to carry the 1," she said, pointing to some scribble on the ledger. "And then, you transposed this number on the spreadsheet. It's supposed to be a 7, although it *does* look like a 9."

Her mom tilted forward, adjusting her glasses, and laughed. "You're so right! I've been struggling with this for an hour, and you solved it in less than a minute!" She patted her daughter affectionately on the arm. "You should pick up some tutoring!" When Mia groaned loudly, she removed her glasses, her eyes growing bright. "What, sweetie? What did I say?"

Mia revealed the envelope, handing it to her mom. "Looks like you're not the *only* one."

Chapter 5

"Just. One. More. Minute," Mia whispered at the oven door. Her eyes remained fixed on the full sheet pan of biscotti with her nose almost pressed against the glass. Like a hawk stalking its prey, she never wavered.

With a *whoosh*, the kitchen door swung open, and her mom burst in, hands-on-hips. "Mia Antoinette! What is taking so long? Look at the clock. You have visitors."

Mia raised her index finger for only a second while pulling the sheet pan from the oven and took a deep inhale of sweet cinnamon, nutmeg, ginger, and cloves. Holding the pan within inches of her eyes, she inspected the result, grinning broadly. As her gaze moved to the clock on the wall, her smile faded. "Shoot! Sorry, Mom. The dough was wetter than I expected. No idea why." When her eyes returned to the sheet pan, she was once again lost in her own world of biscotti.

"Mia," her mom said sternly, trying to regain her attention. "You need to clean up this mess, and yourself, before your father gets back."

For the past two hours, Mia had the run of the kitchen, her dad spending his Saturday morning dropping off deliveries and shopping at the kitchen supply store. Her mom had managed to conspire with her, adding a few more items to his list to keep him occupied.

Mia hurriedly scooped up the hefty container of flour. Spinning on her heel, she tripped over her own two sneakered feet and launched the contents everywhere. As a plume of fine powder enveloped Mia and the room like a bomb, her mom desperately tried to stifle her laughter.

"This... is *not* funny," Mia huffed, brushing the thick film off her apron.

When the whiteout had cleared, Mia's mom stepped forward to rescue her from the flour explosion, sifting it off her hair. "You, my dear, are absolutely covered. Go and clean yourself up, and I'll *try* to find the floor." With flour particles still suspended in the air like pixie dust, she took a long look around and sighed. "Or maybe I'll level the place and start over." As Mia exited the kitchen in a long line of snowy footprints, she couldn't help but join in her mom's laughter.

Mere moments later, Mia emerged from the kitchen, still trailing flour with every step. She'd managed to wind up her hair into a messy bun and remove her caked apron. But, for all intents and purposes, she still resembled a ghostly train wreck.

It was easy to spot her visitors in the sparsely filled bakery. A tall gentleman was keenly dressed in an expensive, freshly pressed suit and long dress coat—all in black. He stood with pristine posture, albeit uncomfortably, in front of the long counter. Of course, beside him, carrying his messenger bag and a scowl was Bryce. Mia approached them with a welcoming smile and could swear she saw a hint of Bryce's dimples as he looked up to her dusty appearance.

"Hello, Mr. Fitzgerald. Sorry to keep you waiting. I'm Mia." She offered her hand, still dripping flour. The gentleman stared down at her hand, unsure what to do with it. Scanning her from head to toe, he was obviously reconsidering his decision to trust his son's GPA and potential football career on this calamity of a human being.

As he continued to stare, the kitchen door abruptly swung open, revealing Mia's mom's more professional appearance. She extended her clean hand to the gentleman. "Lovely to meet you. I'm Mia's mom, Emery. Please, make yourself at home."

The gentleman briefly shook her hand, leaving Mia's still hanging in the void. "Thank you. I'm Carter Fitzgerald, Bryce's father." He barely gave his son a nod as he placed his hand firmly inside his pocket. Mia shrugged and did a mental eye roll, wringing out her floury hand and wrapping it tightly behind her back.

"Let me get you a cup of coffee, and we can discuss—" Mia's mom started, moving forward.

"That's quite all right. I need to get to the office," Carter interrupted, pulling his cell phone from his pocket.

On a Saturday? Mia thought. She caught Bryce roll his eyes.

"I'll return for Bryce in two hours. That should be acceptable, no?"

Mia gave another shrug. "Well, I haven't really looked at the assignments, so I'm not sure..." When she saw her mom's raised eyebrows and bright eyes, she instantly regretted her candor. "I mean, sure. Two hours is perfect." Carter coolly patted his son on the back before rushing out with his phone to his ear.

As Mia steered a silent Bryce over to a quiet corner of the bakery, she noticed his less formal appearance of dark jeans, hunter-green sweater, and dark brown dress shoes. But even that was quite a contrast to her own faded blue bakery t-shirt and now dusty jeans and sneakers.

With a loud *clunk*, Bryce dropped his bag halfheartedly onto the table. Immediately, Mia spotted an insignia consisting of a gold laurel wreath enclosing an ornate shield. A massive deep burgundy "W" was located dead center. She had no doubt this was the Wellington crest, and her interest was piqued. Why did Bryce still carry his old school's bag?

"Here, sweetie," her mom said with a wink, leaving Mia's backpack, two water glasses, and a warm plate to break the ice. As she walked off, she made a motion to her cheek that her daughter instantly ignored.

Practically bursting with excitement, Mia offered Bryce the plate. "Would you like one?"

Giving it a passing glance, he wrinkled his nose. "What's that?"

"It's gingerbread biscotti. I just made them. Been trying to perfect the recipe all week, and now I think it's solid, for the most part." She pushed the plate closer, beaming.

But he waved it off. "No, thanks. I don't eat sugar."

Taken aback, she stared, then laughed off his comment. "You must be joking? Here—try one." When he waved it off yet again, her smile faded. "Oh-kay. Sor-ry," she said, under her breath.

"What's the assignment?" was Bryce's sad excuse for small talk as he cracked open his algebra book.

Mia pushed her rejected biscotti to the side and searched her bag for her book and the notes from Mr. Thompson. Her basic task was to get Bryce "up to speed" and "quickly" in both science and algebra. But she still wasn't sure what that was going to entail. Giving the instructions a quick skim, she nodded. "Okay. Looks like you were a few chapters behind at your old school. How about we start here?" She flipped his algebra book to page 38, pointing to the first problem.

Bryce reluctantly started scribbling something with his pencil. "You have flour on your face," he said flatly, his eyes never leaving his notebook.

Mia felt her cheeks go blazing hot as she lifted her hand to remove the stray flour. She vowed not to ignore her mom's prodding next time. Shaking it off, she tried to change the subject. "So, why'd you leave Chadwick?" When Bryce looked up, the expression on his face made it clear, her question was *not* the right icebreaker. Ignoring her, he returned his focus to his notebook for the remainder of their tutoring session.

Two hours couldn't pass fast enough for both tutor and student (at least they could agree on *something*). Grateful for the sound of the shop bell as the Fitzgeralds disappeared out the door, Mia buried her head in her hands, her *groan* echoing throughout the bakery. Nothing—not even Bryce's boarding school scoop—was worth this aggravation!

Her mom patted her on the shoulder as they heard a booming voice from behind the swinging door. "What the heck happened in here? It looks like a bomb went off!" Mia and her mom shared a look, then broke into hysterics at the forgotten mess in the kitchen.

Chapter 6

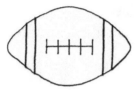

After spending the morning cooped up and miserable behind her algebra book, Mia desperately craved some fresh air and exercise. When she asked her friends to meet up at their favorite park near the bakery, Zach was the first to show, eager to warm up his throwing arm.

"Come on, Mia. It couldn't have been that bad," he said, from the opposite end of the lush, green lawn. "Bryce seems like a great guy on the field. And he was amazing at last night's game." Zach hurled the old football high into the air, across the length of the small park.

Catching the ball with ease, she grumbled, "Well, since he's your new bestie, why don't *you* tutor him?" She threw him a stern gaze, along with another perfect spiral.

"Hey, I'd consider it if I was any good at math. And definitely, if it would stop you from being such a grump." Needing a breather, he waved Mia over to the closest bench, framed by the reddish-orange foliage of a mature maple.

"Sorry. He just *gets* to me." She pulled her usual plastic tub from her bag, snapping open the top. "And you'd better not tell me you suddenly don't eat sugar."

"Don't eat sugar? How weird is that?" Zach eagerly dug his hand into the container.

"Precisely." She perked up a tad and spotted Harper and Chloe rounding the entrance of the park.

"Ooh. What's today?" they heard as Chloe made a bee-line toward the container, sticking her nose inside. "Mmm. Cinnamon."

Mia sighed dramatically. "Only gingerbread biscotti that's apparently not worth the calories," she moaned.

"Huh?" Chloe gave her a look, diving into the molasses-colored cookies.

"Ignore her. She's just bummed about her new tutoring gig," Zach said, taking more biscotti and waving it in the air. "These are delicious, by the way, Mia."

Harper brushed some dry, expired leaves off the wooden bench and sat down. "So, any new details on the boarding school front?" Mia's side-eye to Harper indicated it definitely was the wrong question to ask so soon after her glum Bryce encounter. "Never mind. Anyway, Mia. Thoughts on the school charity project for this semester? As freshman class president, it's your job to come up with some ideas."

Mia thoughtfully chewed on her cookie. "Hmm. I've gone back and forth about a few things. The food bank is an awesome charity. Local and such a great cause."

As vibrant leaves tumbled and swirled around them like confetti, Zach tossed the football over his head. "Totally. I could get the team involved, too," he said between cookie bites.

"Does everything have to be about the football team?" Mia caught the ball mid-toss and playfully ran from Zach.

He caught up to her as she turned and threw it back. Cradling the ball under his arm, he bent over to catch his breath. "Seriously, Mia. You think you could give Bryce a bit of a break?"

She shot a narrowed look at her best friend. "What do you mean? He's the obnoxious one."

Zach paused, pondering how to respond. "I think it's, well, complicated."

"Complicated?"

Hesitating, he pushed out a long exhale. "Well, being starting quarterback as a freshman on our losing team isn't exactly a walk in the park. Especially when most of our upperclassmen dropped out of the offensive line," he said, shaking his head to himself.

Mia took the opportunity to snag the ball out of his hands. "That's not complicated, Zach. You still have a pretty experienced defense. And, with your catching, Logan's kicking, and ... Bryce ..." She tried to squelch a grimace—this was becoming a habit. "It sounds like a winning recipe to me."

Zach raised his chin to the puffy, cotton-ball clouds of early autumn, looking pensive. When he continued, his voice was lowered and apprehensive, as though he was reluctant to spill a secret. "A few of the guys were talking. Bryce left Chadwick, um, *quickly.* We don't know the details, but it couldn't have been on good terms. Anyway, it seems like he's had a rough time lately." Mia spun the ball in her palm, still looking unsure. "Come on, Mia. If anyone can give him the benefit of the doubt, it's you."

Backing up and throwing him a smile as tight as her spiral, she mumbled, "No problem, Zach," but doubted it would be that simple.

Chapter 7

The next Saturday, Mia was busy polishing the glass display cases when Bryce walked into the empty bakery. She greeted him with a friendly smile, like she'd done every day that week. Despite being a model quarterback and winning them yet another game the night before, he still wasn't the model lab partner by any stretch of the imagination. But, with Zach's words replaying in her head, she was determined to give it her best shot.

"Hello, Bryce," she said cheerfully, hoping it didn't sound too forced.

He waved, looked around, then made a face. "Where is everyone?"

Mia fidgeted with her rag, shifting her weight from one sneaker to the other. "Um, well, it's the afternoon. The mornings are our busiest times." While that was true for most bakeries, the real truth was that lately, any hour the DeSalvo Bakery was open was a slow one.

"Oh," he said, not looking convinced. "You know that brand-new coffee house around the block is full." He leaned back toward the window, gazing down the street. "I just walked by, and you can barely get through the door."

Mia pursed her lips. Did Zach have any clue how difficult his request was? "Anyway, I'll grab my books, and we can get started. Clearly, my mom can take care of 'everyone' on her own," she said, a hint of annoyance in her voice.

"You got Wi-Fi?" he asked, laying his tablet on the closest table.

She tried to hold her patience. This very topic had been a sticking point only a couple of days ago. "No," she grumbled.

"Seriously?" He looked amused. "Why?"

"My dad says you should sit and chat while enjoying your coffee or food. You shouldn't be on your 'devices.'" She struggled to keep the bitterness in her tone to a minimum.

Bryce picked up his tablet, giving her a curious look. "That's a nice idea, but just not practical."

Mia regarded him for a moment, realizing for the first time that Bryce was making complete sense. "Um, yeah. We have Wi-Fi in our place upstairs." She motioned him to follow her to the back of the bakery.

When they'd reached the staircase, he looked up with trepidation. "Really? You live up there?"

Narrowing her eyes, she folded her arms over her bakery t-shirt. "Yeah. So? Is that a problem?" Bryce shook his head, clearly not wanting to antagonize her further.

Without uttering another word, she led him up the creaky flight of stairs, pushing open an old, nondescript wooden door. The apartment was spacious, with bright colors, eclectic artwork, and comfy furniture. The centerpiece was a large, gourmet kitchen filled with industrial appliances and stainless steel. It opened up to a substantial eating area, including a large, round marble table surrounded by sleek, soft velvet chairs in burnt orange.

"This is awesome," Bryce said, and Mia's eyes and temperament softened.

"You can drop your stuff here and take a seat. I'll be right back." She patted the marble table before running off to her bedroom.

She returned seconds later with her brimming backpack and Bryce still standing. He waited as she flopped into a chair, finally taking a seat himself. Throwing her bag onto the table, Mia unzipped it, pulling out stacks of papers in her neat penmanship. "Hmm. Where did I put that assignment from Ms. Marsh?" she mumbled, piling several more papers on top of the stack and topping it with her blue science binder. Bryce watched this scene with bemused interest, starting to snicker.

"What's so funny?" she asked, her eyes darkening.

Finally, controlling his laughter, he answered, "You. You're an absolute mess." With Mia giving him a less-than-amused look, he coughed. "Um, no offense."

"Offense taken," she said, through gritted teeth. She crossed her arms, leaning back into her chair. "I have a system. It works."

"You sure?" He picked up a few of the loose papers and waved them in front of her. "Where's the assignment from Ms. Marsh?" Dropping the papers with a smirk, he crossed his own arms.

Mia groaned, pushing back from the table. "I need a snack and a *minute*. I'll be right back."

Leaving a surprised Bryce, she scurried back down to the bakery, sweeping past her mom, chatting with Mrs. Rossi. In the kitchen, she found her dad placing fresh cannoli shells on a tray. When his daughter slid beside him, his face lit up. "Hey, kiddo. How's it going up there?"

She propped her elbows on the stainless counter. "It's not. I came down for a snack and some *less judgmental* air."

Her dad's eyes sparkled. "I have the perfect thing to help with that."

A few minutes later, Mia padded up the steps, armed with reinforcements (she hoped). When she entered the apartment and wandered over to the table, she almost gasped. Bryce was slouched down in his chair with a proud grin plastered all over his face. The messy pile of papers had been replaced with only Mia's single blue binder. "What did you do?" She took a seat and thumbed through the color-coded contents. "And how long was I gone?"

"Long enough," he said, still smiling. "And it was easy with the holes already punched."

Mia lifted the shiny, colorful tabs of green, blue, yellow, and red with the tip of her finger. "Um, what are these?"

He flipped through the pages of her binder. "These separate your papers into sections. You have 'Notes,' 'Homework,' 'Quizzes,' and 'Tests,' which are annoying, by the way."

She looked up from the binder with a critical eye. "Annoying?"

"Yeah. Do you ever get anything other than an A? Seriously, you don't even have an A-minus in the bunch."

Mia slammed the binder closed, nearly crushing his fingers between 'Quizzes' and 'Tests.' "If you *must* know, Bryce, *most* people think good grades are a *good* thing. And I have better things to do with my time than ..." Mia stopped herself, not wanting to say something she'd regret. Taking a steadying breath, she reached for the plate her dad had prepared. "I know you 'don't eat sugar,' but would you like to try ..." She paused once again, seeing his bulging eyes.

"What is that?" he asked, unable to tear his gaze from the plate.

Mia giggled. "You've never seen cannoli before?"

"No, I know that. But the green stuff on top. It, um, looks familiar."

"Oh. It's pistachio. Wait. Don't tell me you have some tree nut allergy or something," she moaned, dropping the plate back onto the table.

But Bryce shook his head, his eyes getting even larger. "No. Um, it's my mom's favorite," he said softly.

"Oh, you must try it then." Mia circled the table and returned from the depths of the kitchen with a knife. Passing him some cannoli, she raised her chin high. "These are our bakery's specialty, from my great-great-grandmother's recipe."

She waited with bated breath as Bryce hesitated, then popped it into his mouth.

Anxiously squirming in her seat, she watched him slowly chew every last morsel. Finally, he proclaimed, "Wow. That *was* good. Especially the pistachio."

Mia was practically humming when she opened her now orderly binder. "So, Newton's third law of motion..." she started, unable to contain her beaming grin.

Two hours later, she was shocked by how quickly the time had gone. Surprisingly, Bryce seemed receptive to her teaching, even allowing her to check his work when they'd reached a tricky algebra problem. When they made their way back down to the bakery, they both were wearing genuine smiles on their faces.

Bryce was heading for the door when Mia exclaimed, "Hold on one sec, okay?" She returned carrying a small, white cardboard box, with "DeSalvo Bakery, since 1919" stamped in deep blue lettering and tied up in red and white baker's twine. Grinning proudly, she presented him with the box.

He simply stared. "What is it?"

"Some cannoli-to-go. With pistachio. For your mom."

As she pushed the box toward Bryce, he said, "No, thank you," his gaze shifting uncomfortably to the tile floor. He paused for what seemed like an eternity, then finally lifted his hazel eyes. But now, they were glassy and colorless, having lost their brilliant light. Holding the box in mid-air, Mia's face fell. Her formerly elated expression was now a mixture of confusion and hurt until he added in barely a whisper, "My mom passed away a few months ago."

Like a swift punch to her gut, Mia's breath caught as her jaw dropped to the floor. Without another word, Bryce turned toward the door, walking out in a *whoosh*. She tried to suck in some oxygen, but it was as though he'd taken all the air in the room with him. So, Mia just stood there, speechless, hugging the box tightly to her chest.

Chapter 8

The next day, three pairs of twinkling eyes peeked through the front window of Urban Coffee. "If your dad finds out about this, he's gonna tar and feather us," Chloe whispered.

"What?" Mia hissed, looking at her like she was crazy. "Stop being so dramatic, Chloe!"

Harper shook her head. "Ignore her, Mia. She's been watching way too much History Channel."

Chloe shrugged. "I'm just sayin'. He's not gonna be happy about this."

"Thanks for the brilliant deduction, Sherlock," Mia said sarcastically.

"Ahem. Can I help you with something?" Six eyes looked up at a face of freckles, wearing a curious expression and an immaculate green apron. According to his nametag, he was "Seth" and had an impressive head of red hair, the exact shade of Little Orphan Annie. He was carrying a full tray of tiny cups holding scant amounts of liquid and offering them to anyone passing by.

Chloe stood up and admired his tray. "Ooh. What do you have there?" she asked cheerfully, rubbing her palms together in delight.

He produced a grin worthy of a salesman on commission, pushing the tray toward her. "Chai latte. It's our special for today."

Beaming, Chloe grabbed a cup and drained it in one motion. "OMG! This is awesome!"

Harper slapped her hand to her forehead. "Geez, Chloe! Deep cover. Remember?" Giving in, she took a cup for herself. "It *is* really good, Mia."

Mia sighed heavily and folded her arms over her sweatshirt, refusing the tray. "The question is—how are the pastries?"

"Won't know until we try," Harper said with a shrug. "Hey, Seth!" Snapping her fingers, she quickly grabbed the green apron's attention. She scanned the area, then passed him a five-dollar bill under his tray. "Bring us your top-selling pastry and, uh, keep the change." Seth stared at the money, gave his head a shake, and ran inside.

Mia darted her eyes around the block, anxiously waiting for Seth to return. When he reappeared a few minutes later, he handed Harper a brown paper bag and a napkin and resumed his sample duties. "What is it?" Mia asked nervously.

Harper shoved the napkin into the bag. As everyone held their breaths, she pulled out a chocolate croissant, large enough to feed an entire family. She held it up to her nose and inhaled deeply. "Holy crap, boss. This. Smells. Amazing!"

As Mia angrily ripped off an edge of the croissant, airy flakes shot in all directions. She chewed for a moment and took a hard swallow while her friends eagerly looked on. "It *is* amazing," she conceded, slumping her shoulders, looking miserable. Pivoting, she started back toward the bakery. "This is a disaster. How are we gonna compete with *that*?"

"Well, at least you know what you're up against," Harper said, lifting the crescent-shaped pastry into the air.

Chloe snagged another corner of the croissant. "You know what they'd say in the nineteenth century—'fight fire with fire.'"

Harper rolled her eyes. "Oh, good grief, Chloe. Lay off the TV for a night."

"That's it!" Mia exclaimed, stopping so abruptly her friends nearly slammed into her back. As she spun around to face them, a mischievous grin formed on her face. "It's time we do some fighting." Taking the croissant, she proclaimed, "And, if we wanna win, we're definitely gonna need this."

Chapter 9

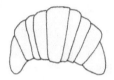

When Zach walked into the bakery kitchen later that night, Mia's eyes were mere inches from the croissant, examining every buttery layer. "Your mom let me in ..." he started. "What the heck are you doing?" he asked with a laugh.

Her eyes never leaving the croissant, she answered, "I'm fighting fire with fire. Or is it beating them at their own game? I honestly can't remember anymore." Lifting her gaze, she threw up her hands. "Or trying anyway."

Zach looked amused, shrugging off his jacket. "What exactly does that mean?"

"Never mind," she grumbled, pushing the croissant away. "I had this great idea, or at least I thought so, until I learned what laminating dough entails. According to YouTube, I'm gonna be up all night." She pointed to her laptop. As the video went in and out, finally freezing, she banged on the side of the screen, then scrolled through her phone. "Stupid Wi-Fi hotspot doesn't work."

"No luck getting your dad to agree on Wi-Fi, huh?"

Mia wrinkled her nose, the subject a bit touchy at this point. "That reminds me. I wanted to ask you something."

He lounged on one of the metal stools. "Fire away."

She grabbed a tray of fresh almond biscotti and offered it to Zach. Taking the stool beside him, she hesitated, nibbling on a cookie. But she knew if anyone understood, it would be Zach. "Does it bother you when people ask about your dad?"

It had been only two years since he'd lost his dad, fighting overseas. Mia would never forget the day the uniformed officers knocked on his front door while she was visiting. His life was never the same, and their friendship grew even stronger.

Waiting a moment to digest her question, his green eyes softened. "I guess it depends. But for the most part, it's nice to remember."

Mia continued to nibble, deep in thought. As her gaze moved to the old football comfortably perched on the shelf, then fell on the cookie tray, her lips curled upward. "I remember your dad loved our almond biscotti."

Zach matched her smile, savoring another cookie. "As do I." When she looked pensive once again, he asked in a hushed tone, "Mia, what's this all about?"

She shook away her thoughts. "Nothing. Just got a lot on my mind."

"I see that." He leaned in to view Mia's screen that had finally stopped buffering. "Since when do you make croissants?"

She sighed. "Since it became Urban Coffee's best seller."

"Well, it's huge," he said, giving the giant pastry a closer look.

"Yeah, and that's not the half of it, literally. And it's amazing. Have you tried one?"

Zach took a small bite from the pastry. "It's pretty good. But honestly, it's nothing compared to your creations." Suddenly, he jumped off his stool and started pacing around the kitchen. "Mia, I think you might be looking at this all wrong."

Intrigued, she stood and followed him around the room. "What do you mean?"

"Well, you're trying to beat them at *their* own game. Why not beat them at *your* own game—from *your* playbook? They say the best defense is a good offense."

With a *groan*, she massaged her forehead. "Seriously, Zach? Way too many football references this late at night. And what does that even mean anyway?"

Zach drew up the zipper on his jacket, grinning as he headed for the door. "You'll figure it out, Mia. Do what you do best, and you can't lose."

Waving goodbye, Mia gave the croissant one more glance. "A good offense? Do what I do best?" she muttered. Then, she cracked a smile as her eyes drifted to the top shelf at the far end of the room.

Chapter 10

O ver here, Mia!" Harper yelled as her friend angled her way through the crowded bleachers on Friday night.

"Thanks for saving the seats," Mia said, finally reaching Harper. "I was afraid we'd end up in the nosebleeds. Where's Chloe?"

"Getting some nachos or something. How'd the meeting go? We thought you were going to miss kickoff."

"I know! But at least we agreed on the charity for the fundraiser. So, food bank, it is!"

"Awesome!" Chloe said, collapsing beside Mia with a gigantic tray of nachos. "Want some?" Mia and Harper wrinkled their noses, then refocused on the game.

"Hey, Zach!" Mia shouted with a wave. He waved back and slipped on his helmet, joining the offense on the field.

"You missed the introductions," Harper said. "Bryce has quite the following already after only a couple games. I swear half the cheerleaders are in love."

Mia shrugged. "Typical. I'm not surprised, though. And he *can* be pretty decent."

Harper did a double take. "What? Is this Mia DeSalvo talking right now? I thought you couldn't stand the kid?"

"Tutoring must be going *really well*," Chloe teased, nudging Mia. "I totally don't blame you, by the way. Those dimples are to die for!" Forgetting her nacho tray, Chloe's twinkling eyes were trained on Bryce as he huddled everyone up for the next play.

Mia did a mental eye roll, ignoring her friends. Since Saturday, she'd had only minimal interaction with Bryce, mostly involving science lab instructions and the occasional lame attempt at small talk. But, with his tutoring session happening the next day, she was apprehensive about once again putting her foot in her mouth.

Changing the subject, Harper asked, "So, anything new on the chocolate croissant front?"

Mia beamed with excitement. All week long, she'd spent her spare time working on her "good offense," and each time, she'd offered the results to her friends. "If all goes well, one more trial run is all I'll need. Here's hoping."

"Well, I'll tell you one thing, boss. If you eat enough of those things, yeah, not so amazing anymore."

"Sorry about that, Harper. But thanks for being my fearless taste testers. And, by the way, I totally agree." Mia giggled, then was pulled back into the action when Bryce rushed for a touchdown.

They sprang from their seats, cheering as the offense jogged off the field. "Great job, Bryce!" Chloe screamed.

When Bryce took off his helmet and turned toward them with curious eyes, Mia slouched down, hiding behind the crowd in front of her. But, with Chloe waving frantically with her non-nacho-tray hand, they were easy to spot. Bryce casually waved, making brief eye contact with Mia, who now felt compelled to wave back.

"Sit down, Chloe," she hissed, tugging on the bottom of her friend's jacket.

Chloe sat down with a mischievous grin. "So, *someone* got a wave from the star quarterback."

Crossing her arms, Mia muttered, "Oh, good grief. I knew I should've spent the night in the bakery." When she cut her eyes back to the field, Bryce had returned to the line of scrimmage and was already moving the Eagles toward the end zone for yet another touchdown.

And that's exactly how things progressed for the rest of the night. By the end of the last quarter, the Eagles had easily outscored the Raiders 43 to 7. The spread would have been even greater had Coach Warner not given Bryce a break and put in the second string to replace him.

Following the rest of the elated crowd down to the field, Mia and Harper found Zach slapping backs and smacking helmets with his teammates. "Hey, guys! Thanks for coming!" he exclaimed as they approached.

Mia offered him a congratulatory hug. "Of course, Zach. Amazing to get on a winning roll. Oh, and great catch there in the third quarter."

"Thanks, Mia. Bryce is the only person I know who can throw a better spiral than you." Her eyes narrowed, and he let out an uncomfortable laugh. "I mean, as good of a spiral. Um. Where's Chloe?"

"She's probably fighting the cheerleaders to get to Bryce by now," Harper joked.

As if on cue, Chloe came bounding in, dragging along a wide-eyed Bryce. "Zach! Sweet touchdown!" she exclaimed with a high-five, then turned to Mia. "I was just telling Bryce about your awesome passing game. Maybe you could help him *practice* sometime."

Mia sneaked a glance at Harper and Zach, who were trying to stifle their laughter over Chloe's obvious strategy. Not amused, she turned to a seemingly intrigued Bryce. "Yeah, well, I'm pretty busy, so you'll have to settle for Zach's sub-par throwing."

Bryce revealed a hint of his impressive dimples as he folded his muscular arms across his navy jersey. "Too bad. I was looking forward to seeing more of that."

As everyone stared, clearly enjoying the show, Mia replied, "Anyway, we should probably get going," starting to drag Harper and Chloe away. "Good game. See ya later." Stumbling off the field, she peered over her shoulder at Bryce, still staring at her with a curious look. It was clear any awkwardness with him was far from over.

Chapter 11

"Mia! Mia, your biscotti is burning!" Snapping awake and leaping from her chair, Mia turned to see her mom chuckling with Bryce right behind her in their apartment kitchen. His dimples had emerged as he clearly was trying to curb some laughter. "I'm sorry, dear. But I couldn't wake you. What are you doing up here?"

Mia yawned and trudged to the fridge, pulling out her buttery dough, carefully stacked like a book. "I was waiting for the final rest on my lamination. It should be ready by now."

"Well, Bryce is here, patiently waiting. I need to get back down to the bakery, so you two have fun." She patted him on the shoulder, then disappeared on the other side of the door. But one glance at Bryce and "patiently waiting" was the exact opposite of how Mia would describe him.

"Sorry about that. I haven't gotten much sleep this week," she said, facing her back to him. With a *grunt*, she started rolling out the dough into a perfect rectangle using an old wooden rolling pin.

Bryce succumbed, abandoning his bag on the marble table. He walked up to the counter, watching her intently. "What are you making?"

"A kind of croissant, but softer and sweeter…and hopefully better. I've almost perfected it… I think," she said breathlessly, her head lowered to her task. "This is laminated dough. Basically, I've folded butter several times into the dough. It creates steam when baked, lifting it into crispy layers, like puff pastry." When her flawless rectangle was complete, Mia, winded from her efforts, proclaimed, "That should work." Using a pizza wheel, she carved fine lines through the dough, creating several equal triangles as Bryce stood by, mesmerized. "Hey. Why don't you wash your hands, and you can help?"

Bryce hesitated, then headed over to the sink. When he returned, he continued to look on, speechless, while Mia laid out the pieces of dough on a sheet pan. "Here," she said, offering him a bowl. "Put one small piece on each triangle."

He timidly took the bowl and lifted it to his nose. "What is this?"

"Dark chocolate. It's so much better than milk. Try some."

Once again, Bryce hesitated, then took a small bite. "Wow. That's intense. Pretty good, though." After he'd placed the chocolate on each triangle, Mia pulled one toward her, rolling it into a horn-shape.

As he continued to study her intricate movements, she asked, "You wanna try?" Without waiting for his answer, Mia pushed a triangle toward him. "Here—like this." She demonstrated the correct way to roll the dough, with Bryce mimicking her instructions to perfection. "Excellent job. Then, we put an egg wash on before letting them proof, or rest, for a couple of hours."

"You mean, after waiting around all that time, you have to wait, again?" he asked incredulously.

Mia smiled. "Yup. But good things come to those who wait." She reached around Bryce and grabbed another sheet pan filled with puffy, rolled dough. "These have already rested, so we just put more egg wash on, add some sugar, and pop them in to bake." His eyes followed her until she slid the sheet pan into the oven. "And then we wait."

"Again," Bryce said with an exasperated sigh. "Where did you learn to do all this?"

She relaxed against the counter. "My dad and mom. YouTube. Trial and error. Urban Coffee," she grumbled, rolling her eyes. "And of course, my great-great-grandma, Antoinette."

"But why? I mean, your parents must do most of the baking, right?"

"Well, yeah. So?"

"Then, why bother? You have more than enough on your plate already. I mean, this seems exhausting, and you barely made it to your first game of the season last night."

"How did you …?" she started. Apparently, any attempt she'd made to hide her late arrival clearly was unsuccessful. But why did Bryce even care? Mia did some mental scrambling, running the question through her mind. Thankfully, she was saved further exploration when the oven timer beeped.

Mia was beyond exhausted when they finally sat down in front of their algebra books and the warm chocolate creations. Bryce cracked a smile, seeing her swiftly locate the still-pristine blue binder from her backpack.

"Here—I thought you'd appreciate this." He pushed a paper in front of her, with a large C+ written in red ink on the top. "My algebra test. Mr. Thompson seemed satisfied."

Mia's deep blues scanned the paper several times, from top to bottom, as she remained quiet. "I know it's not an A, like you, but it should be good enough for football and *most* people."

Mia shifted the test back and forth in her hands. "I guess, but isn't it my job to help you get an A?" While it might be "good enough" for him, it certainly wasn't a glowing mark on her new tutoring gig. It wasn't like she knew how to tutor someone, especially someone as stubborn as Bryce.

"Geez, you're a perfectionist, Mia. It's just one test."

She gave the paper another sweeping glance. "But you don't feel that way about football, right? You never miss a single play. And I'm sure Coach Warner wouldn't want you to be satisfied with giving only seventy-five or eighty percent on the field, right?"

Bryce blew out a hot puff of air, snatching the test from her. "Whatever, Mia. Who really cares? Maybe *you* should join the team, or work for my dad." As he lowered his gaze to his textbook, Mia's stomach lurched. Now, she'd stuck her foot in her mouth, *again*.

Trying to change the subject, she offered him the pastry plate. "Um, want to do the honors?"

"No, thank you," he answered flatly, his head buried in his book.

Over an hour later, when Bryce silently packed up his bag, Mia's mood was as solemn as his. "Thanks, or whatever," he grumbled, heading for the door.

Seeing her last opportunity, she shouted, "Wait, Bryce!" When he swiveled to face her, she pushed a cardboard box into his hands, apologizing the only way she knew how. "In case you want to try them later. Since you helped make them."

Bryce stared down at the box with a look of indifference in his eyes. Grudgingly, he shoved it into his bag. He gave a brief, apathetic wave and left without another word.

Mia collapsed into the soft velvet of her orange chair with her head in her hands. How on earth was she supposed to get anywhere with someone so frustrating? "His mood swings are off the charts," she moaned into her hands.

When she lifted her head a few moments later, her eyes were instantly fixed on something stuck underneath the kitchen counter. Reaching forward to grab it, she came up empty. Letting out a *grunt*, she slid her foot across the floor and farther under the counter, catching the edge of a black and white marble composition notebook. "It must be Bryce's," she said, although she was sure she'd never seen it before. Breathless and flushed, she reached down once more, grabbing the spine of the book as a single sheet of paper fell from its bindings. Immediately, she was drawn to the beautiful penmanship, filling the page from front to back. Once her eyes fell on the paper, she started reading... and didn't stop until the page had run out.

Chapter 12

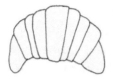

This is incredible, Mia," her mom said, sampling her daughter's newest creation. "I knew you were working hard all week. What's it called?"

Pulling out her cell phone, Mia pointed to a photo of a page in her great-great-grandmother's recipe book. "It's a cornetto. Basically, it's a croissant, but not as buttery or flaky. I experimented with a few things, especially the amount of butter and sugar. And, of course, I added the dark chocolate."

Her mom slipped on her glasses and studied the photo, creases forming on her forehead. "I thought it looked familiar. I think we used to make those years ago. But your improvements will definitely breathe new life into them. You should show your dad, Mia. He'd be so proud."

She shook her head. "We've been through this, Mom. I'm not ready yet." As much as Mia wanted to share her new ideas, she knew how resistant her dad was to change. His unyielding "thanks, but no thanks" echoed in her head like a stuck song on her phone's playlist. If she was going to bring yet another new idea to the kitchen table, she had to make sure he absolutely couldn't say no. "Why did we stop making these and so many other things?"

"Well, your dad streamlined the list over the years to save time or money. Basically, if it didn't sell as much as we'd like, we had to make some tough choices."

Mia understood how tough choices were affecting the bakery. Things were getting redder on their spreadsheets, and she knew they were running out of time.

Later that night, Mia turned down pizza and a movie with her friends, opting for a quiet evening and an early turn-in. After checking the lock on her bedroom door, she scurried to her bed, reaching under her stack of pillows. She pulled out the composition book and stared at its seemingly innocuous black and white cover. Even after only one look, she had a suspicion it was brimming with secrets, maybe even revealing the *real* Bryce. Deep down, she knew it was wrong to intrude on someone's personal thoughts. But, with something so beautifully written and holding so much potential, it seemed impossible to resist.

It didn't take long for Mia to discover that Bryce's talents didn't end on the sidelines. There was no doubt, he also was a gifted writer. And his captivating words soon revealed his departure from Chadwick was not a simple, innocent affair. While she didn't know all the details of the "incident," a good friend of Bryce's and chronic troublemaker, Sebastian, was at the heart of it.

What she found most compelling were Bryce's entries about his mom. Mia, again, didn't know all the details about her passing, but the "C-word" was used frequently. Apparently, she was sick for a short time, but it was intense.

There was no question Bryce was close to his mom and missed her dearly.

As Mia continued to read the intimate passages of his journal, she felt like she was getting to know both its author and his mom a bit better. In this forum, Bryce was brutally honest. But, when she reached one particular journal entry, it became abundantly clear how honest he could be. And what was even clearer, was how Bryce *really* felt about Mia.

Chapter 13

When Mia rolled through the school gates on Monday morning, her mind was still reeling over the composition book. Even as she parked her bike, she felt the weight of its contents crushing her backpack. *This is what I get for being nosy,* she thought, meeting up with her friends.

"Hey, Mia! There you are. Zach was looking for you at the beginning of practice," Harper said, pointing to the football field.

"Sorry. Overslept. I, uh, had a lot on my mind." Mia craned her neck over the fence bordering the field. It was easy to spot Bryce, his nimble legs weaving around the other players as they finished their last play of the morning. "Oh. Here, Chloe. Final result." She offered her a container of cornetti, keeping her attention on the field.

"Ooh, thanks," Chloe said, grabbing the container. Ripping open the top, she took a chocolatey bite. "Oh, wow, Mia. Yeah, these *are* a winner!" Mia absentmindedly nodded, focusing her eyes back on the field.

The team was heading into the locker room before the first bell when Zach ran toward her. "Hey, Mia!" he exclaimed. As she met him by the fence, he passed her the football. "You wanna come throw the ball around with Logan, Bryce, and me at the park after school? We've got a bye week coming up, so Coach is giving us the afternoon off."

Aimlessly twirling the ball around in her hands, Mia focused beyond Zach to Bryce's diminishing silhouette. "Shouldn't Logan be practicing his kicking instead? His last field goal definitely was leaning a bit left," she said, lost in her own thoughts.

"Yeah, well, I'm sure you could give him some pointers later. You game?" When she continued to stare off into space, distracted, he waved his hand in front of her. "Earth to Mia."

Snapping back to the present, she answered, "Sorry. I can't. Have a class council meeting after school to iron out the charity fundraiser." Passing back the football, she casually asked, "How well do you know Bryce?"

"How well?"

"You know, do you guys hang out, or anything?"

Zach raised an eyebrow. "Wow, Mia. You really are out of it. Yeah. Like when we plan to hang out later, at the park? Seriously. What's going on?"

She cleared her throat, stepping away from the fence. "Uh, sorry, Zach. Probably just need to lay off all those croissants. The sugar is clearly clouding my brain," she joked, letting out an uncomfortable laugh. "I'll see ya around, okay?" At the sound of the bell, she waved goodbye, leaving Zach scratching his head as she disappeared inside the building.

Passing the threshold of her science class, Mia had one important task for the hour. But she needed to hold out for the right moment. Taking a steadying breath, she cheerfully marched over to her lab station, greeting Bryce with a friendly, if not ridiculously fake, "Good morning."

He did a double take but answered with a curt, "Hey."

After a detailed lesson on electricity and magnetism, where Mia did her darnedest to pay attention and take notes, Ms. Marsh called everyone up to the front to demonstrate the morning's experiment. When Bryce followed the herd, Mia lingered by their lab station, pretending to search for a dropped pencil. Waiting until Bryce was out of view, she swiftly pulled the composition book from her backpack and slipped it into his Wellington messenger bag. When she finally left her station, Chloe angled her way with a puzzled look. Mia simply smiled, breathing a sigh of relief as she slid beside her in time for the final demonstration.

"Everything okay?" Chloe whispered.

Mia let out a shaky exhale. "Yup. Everything's as it should be."

That was true, at least when it came to the composition book. But as far as things went between tutor and student, it couldn't be more tense. Bryce clearly was still holding a grudge about last Saturday, and Mia was still steaming over his journal's revelations. If only she could find a way out of this tutoring nightmare. In the end, the easiest solution was to get Bryce a few A's and be done with it—and him—for good.

Trudging into the quiet bakery after school, Mia hung her head low. She tossed her bag onto the marble counter with such little enthusiasm, she almost missed. "How was your meeting?" her mom asked.

"Fine. But not definitive. No one can seem to agree on a fundraising activity for the food bank. Today's been disagreeable all around."

Her mom gave her a sympathetic look. "I'm sorry, honey. I'm sure you can bring everyone together and come up just with the right thing. Why don't you go up and rest a bit before dinner? I'll finish cleaning up down here."

"Where's Dad?"

"He's in the study, working on the books. Just follow the grumbling," she said with a wink.

When Mia made her way upstairs to the apartment, yellow light was streaming from inside their study. As she approached the slightly ajar door, she heard her dad sighing repeatedly. Lightly tapping on the door, she popped her head inside. "Hey, Papà," she said softly as his gaze lifted from the laptop screen.

"Hey, kiddo. How's our class president doing?" The glow of the desk lamp highlighted his dark features, leaving Mia's heart to ache. There was a weariness to his espresso-brown eyes, with even darker circles formed underneath them. Still wearing his dusty chef's jacket from a long day of baking, he was slouched down in his chair, clearly not enjoying his task.

"Fine, thanks. How are you?" she asked, already knowing the answer.

Rising from his chair into a deep stretch, he answered, "Done for the night," and bent down to give her a tight embrace and a kiss on the cheek. Before crossing the threshold, he stole one more glance at the desk and a tall stack of menacing envelopes staring back.

A part of Mia wanted to pull out the container from her backpack and offer him her newest creation. She wanted to give him her little notepad full of ideas for the bakery. And, most of all, she wanted to make all those red numbers turn black. But she knew it wasn't that simple.

Heading to her bedroom from the study, Mia pivoted back and gave her dad a supportive smile. "Love you, Papà." His weary eyes softened as he returned his daughter's smile. *If only it was that simple,* she thought. Then, again, maybe it was.

Chapter 14

By the time Saturday morning came around, Mia was glad for a break from school and thrilled to be distracted by mundane bakery tasks. She was collecting Mrs. Rossi's second cappuccino when Bryce strolled through the door. As she looked up to his smirk in full force, her eyes immediately moved to his hand—and a green cardboard cup with "Urban Coffee" printed in obscenely large letters. Mia tried to steady her hands *and* her temper as she carried the cup of cappuccino to Mrs. Rossi's table. "Enjoy," she said, through clenched teeth, trying not to shatter the porcelain saucer on the table.

Signaling Bryce over to a corner of the bakery, Mia whirled around to face him, her intense gaze piercing through him. Crossing her arms with a huff, her olive skin was now heated to a fiery shade of scarlet. "What the heck do you think you're doing?" she snapped.

He shot her a confused look. "What are you talking about?" With her arms still crossed, she simply thrust her chin toward his cup. "So?" he asked, taking a long sip.

Mia tried to suck in some air as her heart rate increased. "You don't think that's even the least bit rude? We sell coffee here, you know. *Fantastic* coffee," she said, her elevated voice shaking.

Bryce did an eye roll, savoring another slow sip. "You need to chill, Mia. Geez. It's just a cup of coffee." But, to her family, it wasn't "just" a cup of coffee. It was their livelihood.

Mia's hands tightened into fists as she reached her boiling point. Stepping within inches of him and his green cup, she raised her voice even higher. "Bryce, has anyone ever told you that you're a pain in the—"

"Mia, dear!" She turned to see her mom only a few feet away. "Why don't you take Bryce upstairs, and you two can work on your next assignment?" Mia's mom moved forward and pushed them toward the back of the bakery. With a stern look, she whispered to her daughter, "We may not have a ton of customers, but I'd like to keep the ones we *do* have."

Mia felt her face burn hotter, but this time not in anger. "Sorry, Mom," she said softly. Her mom gently ushered her up the stairs, watching Bryce grudgingly follow.

Passing the doorway, Mia ripped off her apron, stomping into her room for her backpack. Any remote sympathies or guilt she'd felt for reading Bryce's journal were long gone. When she returned, he was already sitting at the marble table, engrossed in his tablet. She hurled her bag onto the table with such force it shook and then collapsed into an orange chair.

"Wow. You really have a temper, don't you?" he said calmly, seemingly taunting her.

She pulled out her blue binder and tossed it onto the table. "You haven't heard the half of it, so I'd quit while you're behind." Mia easily found Mr. Thompson's assignment, throwing it into his lap. "If you're so clever, why don't you figure it out?"

Despite his wide eyes, he let out a *snort*. "Yeah. Whatever," he said, dropping his algebra quiz into Mia's lap. "Here— another one for you to bellyache about."

The moment she noticed the red B+ on top, her heart sang. *Finally!* she thought, hopeful this ordeal might soon be over. After all, he was only "humoring her," the "absolute mess" anyway, right? At least, according to his own written words. "Wow. It's almost as if you're taking this seriously," she said sarcastically while skimming the quiz.

Taking offense to her comment, Bryce's smirk faded. "You don't think I am?" Mia looked up from the paper with one raised ebony brow. "I'll have you know, Mia DeSalvo. I was a straight-A student, just like you, at my old school— thank you very much. I'm not some dumb jock."

Mia set down the paper, almost laughing. She could hardly believe his words. Since when was he taking *this* or *her* seriously? Challenging him, she crossed her arms and said, "So, what changed then?"

Discomfort flitted across his face, his eyes moving down to his hands. "*Stuff* happened. But it's none of your business."

Lifting the paper amid her most impressive eye roll, Mia blurted out, "Yeah, well, probably because you hang out with people like *Sebastian*." As soon as the word flew out of her mouth, she regretted it. Cringing behind the paper, she wished to turn back time. But when she lowered it slightly and saw the look on Bryce's face, she knew her wish had *not* been granted.

"Excuse me?" His penetrating gaze seared through her paper shield.

Mia clamped her mouth shut, pretending to examine every fine detail of the algebra quiz. *What have I done?* she thought.

Springing to his feet, Bryce snatched the paper from her hands, shoving it into his bag. He paused, then pulled out his composition book and held it mere inches from her bright blue eyes. "Did you read this?" When she remained silent, he yelled, "Yeah, so, *now* you're quiet!"

He stuffed it back into his bag, hightailing for the door as Mia called after him. "I'm sorry, Bryce. It was an accident!"

Turning on the spot, he shot her his best scowl. "What? So, it threw itself at you? Asked to be read?" He pivoted back toward the door. "Whatever, Mia."

"Bryce, please," she begged, running after him. "I found it here, after our last session. Honestly, I didn't mean to read it, but a page fell out." Talking to his back, Mia confessed, "But you're right. It was my choice to *keep* reading." As he faced her, she looked down at her feet in shame. "It was so beautifully written. I've never read anything so *amazing.*"

When she lifted her eyes, his had softened. But, with a deep breath, he said firmly, "We're done here, Mia. *Done*," spinning back around and wrenching the door open.

Watching Bryce storm out, Mia never felt so horrible. Regardless of the awful things he'd written about her, or even thought about her, those were his thoughts alone. She trudged back to her chair, feeling numb all over. As a single tear rolled down her cheek, she couldn't help but wonder if his written words were, in fact, true.

Chapter 15

A couple of hours later, Mia was aimlessly pacing up and down the street in front of the bakery when Zach came into view. Since her blowout with Bryce, she could barely sit still, trying to figure out her next move. When she texted her best friend an SOS that she needed a "guy's insight," he came to the call, no questions asked.

"Hey. Everything okay?" he said as she continued to pace anxiously and chew on her fingernails. She shook her head and took another trip down the block with Zach following. "Come on, Mia. I already did my laps at practice this afternoon."

She halted and did an about-face. "Practice? This afternoon? Was Bryce there?"

"Yeah. Of course. He's the starting quarterback. As a running back, I need someone to throw me the ball." She continued to bite her nail, lost in her own thoughts. "What's this about, Mia? Why all the vague questions about Bryce?"

She pushed out a held breath, her gaze lowered as she toed the sidewalk with her sneaker. "I kinda messed up, badly."

Zach took a seat on the curb in front of the bakery and gestured for Mia to join him. With his eyebrows raised, he listened carefully to her describe her disastrous tutoring sessions with Bryce. And then, she reluctantly shared her mistake of reading the journal. She didn't divulge the details of what she'd read but rather explained how ashamed she was by her behavior. Mia admitted she was drawn to it, and his amazing writing, but she also knew better.

Burying her face in her hands, she muttered, "Zach, I don't know what to do. What I did was unforgivable."

"Of course, it's forgivable. Most things are." As she hung her head low and continued to shake it, he slung his arm around her shoulder. "You're a good person—awesome, actually. Don't get yourself down like this."

"Thanks, Zach. But it's on me to fix this."

"True. You should apologize, again. And I know you don't see it, but Bryce *is* a good guy. We even talked a bit about my dad the other day."

Mia lifted her head, her eyes wide. "Really? Why?"

"Some of the guys mentioned my dad to Bryce since he's wearing his number now. I guess Bryce reminded them of how Dad used to fly by everyone on the field when *he* was quarterback for George Washington."

She smiled. "All-State Champs, right?"

"Yup," he said, matching her grin. "And Bryce mentioned his mom a little."

Mia's face fell. "Yeah. Remind me to tell you how I managed to mess that up, too. Maybe after I've recovered from this disaster, if that's even possible."

"You know the saying, 'you catch more flies with honey'?" he asked in a hopeful voice.

Giving her head a shake, she heaved a heavy sigh. "You're great, Zach. But sometimes you're a bit out-there with the advice."

He laughed. "Well, my dad used to say it, so I looked it up one day. It's from Benjamin Franklin and actually starts, 'Tart words make no friends.' See, Mia, you're a fierce and passionate person, which is awesome. But when you let your guard down to your friends, we also see how kind and generous you are."

"Thank you," she said, her eyes soft.

"No problem. But my point is, let Bryce see all that. Be yourself." When she still looked unconvinced, he clarified, "Accident or not, you found out some really personal stuff about him. Maybe it's time you shared something personal about yourself?"

She nodded, digesting Zach's thoughtful advice. "Kind of like leveling the playing field?"

"Look who's offering up the football references now," he said, nudging her.

Mia rolled her eyes. "Yeah, well, hanging out with you guys, it was bound to happen." She started back toward the bakery. "Come on, you dork. You quoted Ben Franklin for me. That totally deserves some biscotti," she joked as they laughed their way inside.

Chapter 16

Mia parked her bike in front of SkyView Apartments and reached into her pocket for Zach's directions. After confirming the address, she slid off her helmet and scanned the looming, dark glass-paneled high-rise. With a steadying breath, she grabbed her "reinforcements" from the rear basket and headed for the revolving door. Immediately, she was greeted by an older gentleman, attired in a sleek, black double-breasted jacket and matching hat. "Excuse me," she said to the doorman. "Wait. Sal? Is that you?"

"Miss Mia?!" He reached down to swallow her into a giant hug.

"Sal, I haven't seen you in the bakery in ages. Since when did you start working here?"

"Since my 401(k) didn't go as far as I planned," he said with a shrug. "But it's easy work, and the people are nice, so I can't complain. Except missing my morning cannoli."

"Well, you are in luck!" Mia offered him one of her "reinforcements"—a box of cannoli and biscotti. "Help yourself."

Sal dived into the box with gusto. "Wow. Thank you, Miss Mia. What brings you here, of all places? It's a few blocks off your normal route. You delivering now?"

"Nah. Just visiting. My, uh, friend lives here, on the top floor, apparently."

"Oh? The Fitzgeralds?" he asked, between bites. "Bryce is such a nice young man."

Mia did a double take. "Really? I mean, yeah. Sure, he is." She made a mental note—to commit a bit better when she lied.

Licking his fingers, Sal handed back the box and escorted Mia inside an expansive lobby of dark, glittery marble. He waved at another doorman, slumped over the circular front desk with a bored expression. "Hey, Eddy. Watch the door while I take up the lovely Miss Mia to see Mr. Bryce."

Eddy gave her a once-over. "You his girlfriend?"

Mia's jaw fell open. "No! Absolutely not," she blurted out, vigorously shaking her head.

"The door, Eddy," Sal said, pushing him out the revolving door. Turning to Mia, he said, "Ignore Eddy. We all do."

Sal led her down a long hallway to a bank of shiny silver elevators and held open the door. "After you, my dear." Mia walked inside and moved to the back of the cab. The two followed the proper elevator protocol all the way up to the 30th-floor penthouse while the piped-in classical music filled the tight space. When the door chimed and opened, Sal said, "Here we are, Miss Mia. It was wonderful to see you. Give my best to your folks." She hesitated, then gingerly stepped out and waved goodbye. "Have a wonderful night," he added with a tip of his hat.

Now, alone in the quiet, white marble-floored vestibule, Mia was greeted by colossal, dark-stained double doors. Frozen in place, she felt completely out of her element.

Suddenly, it occurred to her she had no idea what she would say to the person on the other side of the elegant doors. What if it was Bryce's dad? He surely wouldn't want to invite her in.

Angling back to the reflective elevator, she checked for any stray flour and smoothed out her long, shiny ponytail. Then, holding her head high and collecting all the courage she could muster, she pressed the brass doorbell quickly before she lost her nerve. As she stood waiting, she tried to calm herself by taking deep breaths and practicing her smile.

Time seemed to stand still until the latch finally clicked, and one of the doors cracked opened to reveal Bryce's wide eyes. They stared at each other in silence while Mia tried to select the proper greeting, after mentally discarding several. Ultimately, she landed on, "Good evening, Bryce. I've come to apologize," with a dazzling, practiced grin, and pushed her peace offerings toward him. He stood there, speechless and rigid, for far too long as her heart plummeted. "Please?" she asked softly, her smile evaporating.

Bryce nodded, fully opening the massive door. She tentatively stepped through the threshold into a wide foyer, defined by a tall arched ceiling, ornate bright white moldings, and deep hardwoods. When he closed the door and turned to face her, she once again pushed her armful of containers toward him. "What is all that?" he asked.

"This large one is some sausage and meatballs from my great-great-grandma's recipe." As he continued to look unimpressed, she blew out a sigh. "And a box of sugar you're probably gonna hate."

"Why do you keep giving me food?"

Mia couldn't help but smile genuinely. "It's my way of apologizing. Kind of grew up with it, so it's all I really know."

Bryce paused for a moment, then reached for the containers. "Follow me."

Passing through the formal foyer, he led her into a spacious living room, filled with luxurious, contemporary furnishings in white linen and dark brown leather. She was awestruck by sweeping views of the city from a large outdoor balcony. A spiral staircase sat in the far end of the room, flanked by a formal dining area and open kitchen with gleaming stainless steel.

Mia paused before crossing the pristine white area rug, kicking off her ratty sneakers in front of an enormous stone fireplace. Bryce slid a glance behind him and shrugged. "Don't worry about it. I drag my football gear through here all the time. Evelyn doesn't care."

"Um, who's Evelyn?" she asked, catching up to him in the kitchen.

"Our housekeeper. She's great." He grew quiet as he placed the containers on the immaculate dark granite countertop.

Mia attempted to fill the silence, pointing to the large container. "You can just heat that up in a pot. It's great for leftovers."

"I don't really cook. That's Evelyn, too."

"Seriously?" She cast a glance across the quiet space. "Is your dad around?"

He shook his head, relaxing against the counter. "Nope. Working late, as usual."

"Do you guys ever have dinner together?"

"Not much since my mom . . . Anyway, I usually just make a sandwich or Evelyn leaves something for us."

Mia nodded, feeling her heart hurt. "Did you, um, have dinner already?" When Bryce shook his head again, she shrugged off her windbreaker. "Okay, then. Where do you keep the pots?"

Chapter 17

T hat was delicious," Bryce said, helping Mia collect their empty plates from the dining room table.

"Nonna Antoinette would be pleased. Except, I forgot the bread. You always have to have bread to soak up the extra gravy."

Bryce met her in the kitchen, looking slightly perplexed. "Gravy?"

"Yeah. You know, tomato sauce." Taking a quick look around the sink, she asked, "Where do you keep the sponges?"

"Mia, you don't have to do the dishes."

"I know. Evelyn probably does that. But I made the mess. And I doubt your dad wants to see that when he gets home, especially if he knows I'm responsible." She started opening the dishwasher, but Bryce reached over and closed it.

"Don't worry about it. I can do the dishes later. I'm not completely helpless."

Mia awkwardly leaned against the countertop, drumming her fingers on the shiny granite. "Well, I should probably let you enjoy the rest of your evening." She grabbed her windbreaker and headed for the foyer, reaching for her shoes along the way. Pausing for a moment, she spun back around. "Listen, Bryce. I came here to say—"

"Are you busy tonight?" he interrupted her.

"Um, no, but I really should apol—"

"Put your shoes on. I have an idea." He moved past her, pulling his jacket and a football from the closet in the foyer.

Mia followed Bryce out the impressive double doors and down the elevator. He took a back exit out of the building and into the crisp night air. "Where are we going?" she asked, continuing to follow him for a couple of quiet blocks.

"You'll see," he said, his dimples visible in the dim light.

Finally, she noticed an emerald glow in the distance. As they approached, Mia's breath caught, unable to believe her eyes. Ahead of them stood a *huge*, grassy park. Located smack-dab in the middle of the darkened city block, it appeared to shimmer. She was giddy as she followed Bryce into an expansive, velvety green field. Turning on the spot, she exclaimed, "This is incredible!"

"Yup. You game?" he asked, handing her the football.

"You bet." She ran to the opposite end of the field and gunned a tight pass directly at him.

When her perfect spiral landed in his hands, he nodded to himself. "I *am* impressed. So, it wasn't just that one time. Zach was right."

"One time?" she asked, catching his throw.

"Yeah. When we first met. I believe you hollered at me."

Mia lifted her chin high, throwing the football. "Because you were rude."

"Gotta work on that temper, Mia. I was speechless from your throw. You almost bruised my hand." The overhead lights bounced off his broad grin as he passed her the ball.

She caught it with a look of surprise in her eyes. "Seriously?" Hugging the football, she jogged up to him. "Tell me another thing, then. Why won't you let me apologize?"

He shrugged. "Because you already have, a bunch of times. And maybe you have your way of apologizing, and I have my way of accepting it."

"So, does that mean you want me back as your tutor?" she asked, tossing the ball up into the air.

Bryce grabbed it, cradling it under his arm. "That depends. You gonna scream at me over a silly cup of coffee?" he teased.

Her expression turned serious. "It's not just a silly cup of coffee, Bryce. Not to me." As he looked on, intrigued, she mumbled, "Remind me to stop asking Zach for advice."

"Huh?"

Mia's gaze moved down to the springy turf as she kicked around a few loose patches. "You figured it out some already, but the bakery's not doing well. In fact, it's pretty bad."

Bryce furrowed his brows as he stepped closer. "How bad?"

"Well, I don't have an MBA or anything, but I'm pretty sure the numbers on a business spreadsheet are supposed to stay positive."

"And Urban Coffee is responsible?"

She looked up and let out a heavy sigh. "Not completely. I mean, it doesn't help. But neither does my father's stubbornness."

"Yeah, well, I guess we have that in common."

For the next hour, Mia and Bryce passed the football, going longer and challenging each other amid constant laughter. When he walked her back to her bike, she teased,

"You know, you should smile more often. The dimples are much better than that smirk you usually give me."

"Thanks a lot. I'll keep that in mind," he said sarcastically.

Mia unlocked her bike and grabbed her helmet from the basket. "Why'd you want to hang out? I mean, after the stuff you wrote?"

"Stuff?"

"You know, the journal. You weren't exactly… complimentary."

Bryce was pensive for a moment, then his mouth formed a coy smile. "Maybe next time you decide to be nosy, you should fully commit."

As he started back toward the building, she shouted, "What does that even mean?"

He spun around, tossing the football above his head. "Mia, try turning the page!"

Chapter 18

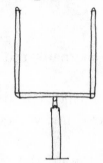

On Friday night, Mia rushed to park her bike and meet her friends at the football stadium. Carrying two plastic tubs toward the stands, she ran into Chloe, waiting in the concession line. "Hey! What's on tap for tonight?" Mia asked, sneaking in line beside her.

"Ooh. I'm thinking fries. Maybe cheese fries. We'll see when we get up there." Noticing the containers, she asked, "So, is that why you were almost late? What's tonight's theme?"

Mia nodded, handing her a plastic tub. "Christmas."

"Christmas? But it's not for a couple more months. You getting a head start?"

"Kind of, I guess." Secretly, she was simply hoping the bakery would be around that long. "So, anyway, it's a combo of pound cake, panettone, and pandoro sweet bread. Basically, it's an Italian Christmas cake."

"Awesome. I love Christmas and cake!" Chloe gushed, moving up the line. "What's with the *two* containers?"

Mia looked around nonchalantly. "Oh, just bringing some to, um, the team. You know, a snack for some energy for the game."

Chloe threw her a smirk. "You mean Zach? Or Bryce?"

"Whichever," she said casually.

"OMG! Mia DeSalvo! You have a *thing* for Bryce! Not that I blame you, by the way."

She shushed Chloe, her eyes darting around anxiously. "I do not! Geez. You're gonna start people talking."

"Well, Mia. Don't think I haven't noticed you two chatting up a storm at your lab station this week. Whatever it is, it's better than you guys arguing."

Mia had to agree. But while she and Bryce were more cordial all week during their lab assignments, despite her continued curiosity, she had opted not to mention the dreaded journal, again.

"Anyway, Chloe. Enjoy your fries, and the cake. I'm gonna go catch up with Harper." She rushed off, grateful to end that topic of conversation.

Strolling along the sidelines, Mia spotted Harper standing in a huddle of blue and gold, including towering Zach and Bryce and petite kicker Logan. Looking up, Zach waved her over. "Hi, Mia! Glad you made it."

"Me too. Here—I baked this for *you guys*. It's cake." She passed the container over to Zach.

"Thanks, Mia. This looks delicious."

Harper checked out the container with an approving nod. "It does look good, boss. Chloe will be thrilled."

"Don't worry. She has her own. I met up with her in the fry line."

Zach elbowed their favorite kicker. "Logan, Mia here has some pointers for you. Apparently, you're leaning left. Right, Mia?"

Bryce's eyes twinkled with amusement. "Hmm. At this rate, we're all gonna be out of a job."

Logan reluctantly agreed. "She's right, though. Coach noticed, too. Been working on it all week. Thanks for the heads up, Mia."

"Anytime. We probably should let you guys warm up. Good luck." Mia patted Zach and Logan on their backs, grabbed Harper, and headed for the bleachers.

"Mia! Wait!" She turned to see Bryce running toward her in his freshly pressed navy jersey, with a striking gold number 5.

Harper perked up, then smiled. "I'll go save us some seats, Mia," she said with a wink.

Mia spun back toward Bryce. "What's up?"

"Are we on for tutoring tomorrow?"

"Oh, yeah. How about two o'clock? Meet me at Urban Coffee."

Lifting an eyebrow, Bryce folded his arms over his chest, highlighting the defined bicep of his impeccable throwing arm. "You're kidding, right? Is this a test?"

"A test?"

"Yeah. Like some kind of loyalty oath? You tell me to meet you there but, in fact, *really* don't want me to?" She shot him a confused look. "Mia, you've made it crystal clear how much you hate Urban Coffee. I heard it. The whole block probably heard it. Why on earth would you want to meet there?"

"Well, tutoring is a good cover for, um, investigating." When he raised his brow another notch, she clarified, "Bryce, I have an idea and need to do a bit of research."

"Okay, Mia. Whatever you say. Two, it is." Just then, Coach Warner blasted his whistle, motioning the team to huddle up.

"Um, good luck out there, Bryce. I'm sure you'll win us another one."

Flashing his biggest grin, he slid on his gleaming gold helmet and ran toward the huddle.

By the time Mia made it to the stands, Chloe had joined Harper, with a super-sized basket of cheese fries. "I don't know where you put it, Chloe. You must have a tapeworm or something," Harper said, shaking her head. Cupping her hand to Mia's ear, she whispered, "So. Looks like tutoring with Bryce *is* going well these days."

"Let's just say we've had our ups and downs."

"I don't know. Seems like you're on a pretty upward trend now," Harper yelled, over the *roar* of the crowd, when Bryce easily moved the ball down the field for a first touchdown.

"We'll see. Honestly, I'm playing it day by day."

"Yeah. Kinda like this team." Harper nervously bounced her knee, waiting for Logan to make his first appearance. "All this winning is great. But I don't trust it."

A few minutes later, Mia found herself holding her breath as Logan attempted his first kick of the night. Apparently, his full week of practice proved fruitful. When the football flew dead center through the goalposts, Harper jumped up, cheering loudly.

"Well, at least we can still trust Logan's kicking," Mia said, blowing out a sigh of relief.

Chapter 19

It was 2:15 when Mia finally ducked into Urban Coffee the next day. Anxiously squinting across the crowded coffee bar filled with dark wooden tables, comfy leather chairs, and a roaring two-sided fireplace, she spotted Bryce relaxing at a small table near the front window. Amid the crackle of grinding beans and caffeine-laden sweet aromas, she weaved her way around the long line of customers and dropped her backpack onto the table. "Hey," she said quietly as he looked up from his tablet.

"Hey, Mia. I was wondering if you chickened out on me." He took a sip from a large porcelain coffee mug and pushed another toward her. "I got this for you."

Hesitating, she asked, "What is it?"

"What every other person in front of me got. I went with the odds—pumpkin spice latte."

She timidly lifted the mug to her nose and then eyes, examining every drop of the frothy orange concoction. "I don't know. I'm more of a coffee purist."

"Give it a try. Consider it research." Bryce watched with curiosity as she took a tiny sip, grimaced, then nodded, followed by another, deeper sip. "Well? What's the verdict?"

"Honestly, I have no idea. One minute I don't like it, the next I do. It's really ... confusing. Definitely would be better with *real* spices, though. Too much synthetic."

"You can tell that from only a couple sips?"

She shrugged. "I guess so."

Bryce laughed as she slid into the chair beside him. "So, what took you so long?"

Mia slouched down behind her backpack, darting her eyes out the window. "Actually, I almost did chicken out. Went around the block half a dozen times. It feels wrong, like I'm cheating on the bakery or something."

"I think that's a bit extreme, Mia. You don't expect to go your whole life never walking into another coffee or dessert place, do you?"

With another shrug, she flipped her long, ebony locks behind her shoulders. "I guess not. Right now, I'm just hoping we're around until the end of the year. Not thinking too far past that." Suddenly, she noticed Bryce staring at her. "What? Am I covered in flour again?"

He shook his head, still examining her. "No. It's just ... I've never seen you with your hair down before. It looks nice."

Her cheeks warmed to match her latte. "Oh. Thanks. Tends to get in the way, so—"

"Chloe? Chloe? Chai latte for Chloe?"

Mia looked up toward the pick-up area in time to see freckled Seth behind the counter holding up a massive, green cardboard cup. "Oh, no, she didn't!" As Chloe cheerfully grabbed her cup and two small bags, a flaming Mia pounded her fists on the table. "Traitor," she hissed, then sprang up.

"Mia, maybe calm down a bit before—" Bryce started.

"Chloe!" she yelled, hands on her hips.

Turning in Mia's direction, Chloe's eyes grew as large as her glasses. She waved meekly, attempting to hide the cup behind her back as she approached their table. "Hey, guys. What brings you here?" she asked casually.

Mia glared at her. "Drop the innocent act, Chloe. You really think we can't see that ridiculously huge cup?"

Giving up on her horrible attempt at nonchalant, Chloe dropped the bags and the whopping 32-ounce cup onto the table and flopped into the closest chair. "Fine. You caught me."

Bryce picked up the cup with an incredulous laugh. "Seriously, Chloe. This is *huge*! What size is this?"

"It's the *Urban Uber*—their biggest size." When Mia narrowed her eyes between the conspicuous cup and Chloe, she added, "I'm sorry. But their chai lattes really are awesome, and you don't make them at the bakery."

Mia blew out some steaming hot air. "Fine. Whatever. I get it. But what is that?" She threw an accusatory finger at the two bags on the table.

"Well, this is a gluten-free muffin for my mom; she's suddenly on a no-carbs kick. And this sugar-free cookie is for my grandpa; he has to watch his sugar levels."

Collapsing into her chair, Mia pouted. "Just great. More stuff we 'don't make,'" she mocked, using air quotes.

"What are you guys doing here anyway? And is that a pumpkin spice latte, Mia? Yum, and *shame* on you," she said, shaking her finger.

Mia groaned and dropped her head onto the table as Bryce answered, "We're doing some research. And you can blame the latte on me. She doesn't even like it."

"Sort of," Mia grumbled under her breath.

Chloe pushed back from the table. "Well, I'd better get going."

"Wait, Chloe," Mia said, lifting her head. "Do they have any cannoli in the case?"

"Cannoli? No way. I think the whole block knows DeSalvo's has that market cornered. But I did hear their cookies are their new best seller. Apparently, all the kids come in for a few to take home or eat on the go, even though they're tiny and crazy expensive. Anyway, you two have fun *studying* . . . or whatever." She gave Mia a wink, then disappeared into a crowd of enormous green cardboard cups.

Mia was thoughtful for a beat before a huge grin formed on her face. "What?" Bryce asked.

"No cannoli, huh? That sounds *interesting*. And like an excellent opportunity."

Chapter 20

Slow down, Mia!" Bryce yelled breathlessly as they raced down the block to the bakery. He caught up with her as she sprinted through the door. "Geez. The heck with football. You ever consider joining the track team?"

Skidding to a stop at the marble counter, Mia deeply inhaled the familiar, calming scents of citrus and vanilla wafting in the air. "Mom! Is Dad out at the store right now?" she asked eagerly, darting her eyes at the swinging door.

"Hello, Mia. I'm fine. Thanks for asking," her mom teased. "Yes. He left a few minutes ago." Without another word, Mia zoomed past her. "While you're back there, dear, you can take the biscotti out of the oven."

Mia was pulling out a sheet pan to cool when Bryce stumbled into the kitchen, still panting. "Yes," she said.

"Um, what?" he asked, scratching his head of tousled waves.

"Yes. Coach Lee wanted me to join the track team. He mentioned hurdles." She set the last hot pan of biscotti on the counter, then started toward the corner of the kitchen. Her sneakers squeaking to a halt, Mia spun back to face Bryce. "Do you think you could, maybe turn around for a sec? It's, well, kind of a secret."

But he remained firmly in place, crossing his arms. "You can't be serious, Mia. You're worried about *me* keeping *your* secret?"

"I know, Bryce. But it's not really my secret to tell. Just a sec, I promise."

"Fine," he grumbled, lifting his palms over his head and turning around.

Mia rushed over to the shelf and climbed the step stool. As she reached for the recipe book, she stole a glance over her shoulder at Bryce, who was still facing his back to her. Once the book was tucked safely under her arm, she jumped down and returned to the counter. "Okay. All set."

Bryce looked far from amused when he ambled over to join her. "What's so important, Mia?" he asked in an annoyed tone.

She clutched the old, tattered recipe book close to her chest, then carefully placed it on the counter. With the tips of her fingers, she slowly traced the detailed cover, outlined with an ornate letter "A." "My great-great-grandmother, Nonna Antoinette, developed all these recipes throughout her life in Italy and passed them down when she immigrated here. Even though she was from Sicily, she traveled all over the country, combining the best of the best."

"This is so cool, Mia." He gently flipped through the treasured family heirloom. "But what are you looking for exactly?"

Unzipping her backpack, she pulled out a small notepad. "When I found out the bakery wasn't doing well, I wanted to come up with some solutions. My dad's not great about change—horrible, actually. So, I thought if I presented a whole plan, maybe he'd take it more seriously. I've jotted down all my ideas and improvements...here." She opened the pad, revealing page after page of her neat handwriting. "I've been working on new recipes—kind of mixing the old and the new. I guess, in a way, Nonna Antoinette and I have been working together."

Bryce smiled, comparing Mia's writing and drawings to those of her mentor. "So, what's your plan now?"

Thumbing through the recipe book, she said, "I just need to find...Wait. Where is it?" Mia flipped back to the beginning of the book and slowly turned each page, brimming with ingredients, instructions, and drawings. When she reached the final page, yet again, she sucked in a few shaky breaths. "Oh, no. It's not here."

"What's wrong?"

Feeling panicky, she started to pace up and down the kitchen. "It's not here. How is that even possible? They're *all* here."

Bryce walked up to Mia and rested his hands on her shoulders to calm her. "What's missing?"

As their eyes met, she answered, "The cannoli recipe. I didn't realize it before, but I've never seen it in the book. I thought this would work. If I could just make the improvements, this could bring them in."

"Well, who knows the recipe? Someone must make them, right?"

A wave of dread swept across her deep blue eyes. She swallowed hard, then croaked, "Just my dad. He's the only one."

"Mia, why don't you ask him? I'm sure he'd want to teach you."

She shook her head, sinking onto the nearby metal stool. "You don't understand. I've only ever seen him make the shells. My mom hasn't even seen him make the filling." Smacking herself on the forehead, she let out a *groan*. "I'm so stupid. How did I not put it together sooner?"

Bryce sat beside her at the counter. "What?"

"He makes the filling in the morning when I'm asleep or gone for school. And only what he needs for the day. In fact, he always pushes everyone out of the kitchen. I assumed it was in the book. I had no idea it was in his head."

"Like a trade secret?"

"I guess. I don't know. It doesn't matter. I'll have to come up with another plan." Mia slid a sheepish glance at Bryce. "Sorry. We're supposed to be doing more fun things, like our assignments."

He let out a laugh. "You think algebra and Ms. Marsh's science lessons are fun?"

With a roll of her eyes, Mia collected her bag from the counter. "Come on. We can work on stuff upstairs."

"Well, recipe or not, your bakery certainly has something going for it that Urban Coffee doesn't."

"What?"

Bryce proudly held up the worn recipe book. "History."

Chapter 21

For the next couple of hours, the diligent duo worked through their long list of assignments. All the while, Mia tried her best to keep her mind off the bakery downstairs. They were finishing the final set of algebra problems when Bryce passed her a sheet of paper. "I waited to give you this, just in case it wasn't quite perfect enough."

She turned it over to view his most recent algebra quiz, revealing a large A- written in red ink. "Bryce, this is incredible! That was a really hard quiz." She threw him a playful jab, her eyes drifting back to the paper.

"Wow. Have I impressed the *perfect* Mia DeSalvo?"

Handing back the quiz, she sighed. "I'm far from perfect. You know that." Pausing for a beat, she bit her lip, then asked, "You said you were a straight-A student before. What happened, exactly?"

Stuffing his books into his messenger bag, he blew out a long exhale. "A lot." He drew in a deep breath, then looked her square in the eyes. "I was at Wellington Prep before my mom got sick."

"Oh?" Mia perked up. This was exactly the conversation she was hoping for. "So, you were at regular private school before transferring to boarding school?"

"Yup. Wellington was awesome. Football was the best. My friends and teachers were great. Then, things changed at home, and my grades started slipping. After my mom passed, my dad tried to stay busy at work. And I guess he didn't know what to do with me because he suggested shipping me off to Chadwick, and that's how it was."

"But you weren't there very long," she probed. When Bryce considered her comment but didn't take the bait, Mia waved it off. "Sorry. Never mind. None of my business." As he focused his attention back on his bag, she added casually, "You just don't seem the type to get into that kind of trouble."

Bryce closed his bag, looking exasperated. "What do you want to know, Mia?"

"Um, nothing," she said innocently, playing with the spine of her book.

With crossed arms, he settled back into his chair. "Mia, just ask. The truth is probably way less interesting than anything you're making up in your head."

She tossed a smirk his way. "So, anyway, you got expelled. What the heck did you do? In less than a month?"

"I broke into a classroom and stole test answers, right out of the teacher's desk." As she stared at him, her mouth agape, he nodded. "Yup. Pretty much the headmaster's same response when he heard. Is that sordid enough for you?" He scooped up his bag and started for the door.

Mia leapt from her chair. "You're gonna leave me with ... with that?"

He shrugged. "What? It's the truth. You wanted to know."

"No, Bryce. That's *not* the whole story. No way."

"Why not?" he asked, recrossing his arms.

"Because. You're smart. You don't need to steal answers. And I don't know you all that well, but you seem to be a good person. Zach vouches for you, too."

Bryce uncrossed his arms, heading toward the door. "Well, Zach is a good guy. Friends help friends."

Mia jumped in front of him before he could move another step. "Is that why you did it? Were you helping a friend?" She thought for a moment, then her eyes lit up. "Were you helping Sebastian?"

Sighing, Bryce ran his fingers through his waves. "Mia, you're impossible. Yes." He moved past her and left with a simple, "See you Monday."

Chapter 22

"You really think he was covering for one of his friends? That guy, Sebastian?" Harper asked, hanging out by Mia's locker on Monday morning.

Mia shoved the last of her books into her backpack. "It makes sense. There's no way he would come up with such a risky stunt on his own. I mean, he put both his academic and football futures in jeopardy. Plus, that kid apparently had gotten in trouble before."

"How'd you know that?" Harper asked as Mia slammed her locker.

The last thing Mia wanted to do was share the journal debacle with anyone else. She was embarrassed enough confiding in Zach. And Bryce certainly wouldn't be happy about it. "Take my word for it. I know."

"So, I guess you and Bryce are on another down of the roller coaster? Geez. I can't keep up."

Mia slung her backpack over her shoulder and started to weave around the packed hallway. "I know. I'm dizzy from it myself. Lately, everything has been exhausting. Which reminds me, have you decided if you want to chair the fundraising committee? You've gotten everyone's vote already."

Harper wrinkled her nose. "I don't know. It's a lot of work. And I have soccer soon ..."

Mia scoffed, pausing in the hallway. "Soccer? Harper, that's not for a few more months. And you practically play year-round anyway."

"Yeah. True. But I've been working with Logan on his kicking in my free time."

Starting to giggle, Mia resumed her walk. "Logan, huh? I'm sure he has more on his mind than field goal strategies."

Harper nailed her with a decent punch but couldn't stop smiling. "Mia! You're awful. I've been friends with him forever."

"Yeah. And he's had a crush on you since kindergarten," she said, stopping in front of Ms. Marsh's classroom. "Anyway, see you later. And just think about the committee." Harper rolled her eyes, turned, and threw a silent wave over her shoulder.

When Mia approached her lab table, Bryce was taking his seat, his face still flushed from the morning's football practice. "Morning," she said, unsure what mood he'd chosen for that Monday.

She figured he must have eaten his Wheaties, because he gave her a bright, "Good morning," with his full dimples.

Mia sent a quick wave to Chloe as she sat down. Then, while waiting for Ms. Marsh to start her lesson, she leaned in toward Bryce. "So, does that pleasant greeting mean you're not mad at me anymore?"

His eyes remained fixed on his book as he said, "I'm not mad at you, Mia."

"You're not?" Suddenly, something occurred to her. "Bryce, are we, um, friends?"

Abandoning his textbook, he faced her. "That depends. Do you want to be friends?"

By his stoic expression, she wasn't sure if he was joking or completely serious. As she contemplated her answer, her teacher started reviewing the information for the next test. Mia shifted her attention to the chalkboard and began taking notes.

A few minutes later, Ms. Marsh passed out a review worksheet to finish between lab partners. Mia approached the assignment in a business-like manner, asking Bryce what he thought of the first question, with her pencil poised and ready.

When they'd finished the worksheet in record time, he asked, "So. Any new ideas for the bakery?" while Mia double-checked their answers.

She shrugged with her head still focused downward. "Um, not really. Not since my cannoli idea failed so miserably."

"What if your idea didn't fail? What if it was a good one?"

Forgetting the worksheet, she raised her chin and her eyebrows several inches. "How so?"

"Well, I was thinking. Who cares if you don't have the recipe?"

"Uh, Bryce. I hate to break it to you. But I can't bake something if I don't have the recipe. I can't just throw a bunch of ingredients together and figure it out."

"Why not? Don't you usually experiment with the recipes anyway?"

Mia propped her head up with her fist, putting her pencil aside. "Well, yeah. But I need an accurate base or something to start from."

"Why not use the actual cannoli as a start? Reverse-engineer it." When she appeared unconvinced, he said, "You did it with the croissant, right? Heck, you figured out the latte from only a couple sips."

"Bryce, are you being serious? You really think I can do that?"

"Absolutely, Mia." As she stared at him, speechless and stunned by his brilliant suggestion, he added, "And you can start on Saturday, at my place."

Chapter 23

Thanks, Sal. See you later," Mia said through the closing doors of the shiny elevator. Walking up to the large,
wooden double doors once again, she rang the bell more
confidently this time. The door opened to Bryce's curious
expression as he gave her a once-over.

"Mia, I could have come down to help you. You didn't
have to lug all that stuff up here by yourself." He gestured
toward the two overflowing cloth grocery bags and stuffed
backpack hanging off her shoulders.

"That's okay. Sal helped," she said as Bryce offloaded the
bags from her arms.

"Sal?" He led her through the doorway and the foyer as
she wriggled out of her windbreaker.

"Yeah. Sal, the doorman. We're really tight. We go
way back."

Bryce chuckled. "Of course, you do. I'm starting to understand the whole class president thing. You could make
friends with the side of a building."

"Why does that sound like a bad thing?" she asked, wrinkling her forehead while following him into the kitchen.

"Trust me. It's not. Sal's awesome."

Mia unpacked the bags filled with sheet pans and kitchen tools, then pointed to the sacks of flour and sugar on the counter. "Thank you for getting all this. I think my dad would've gotten a clue if he saw me dragging bags of flour out of the kitchen."

Bryce cracked a smile. "Well, you can thank Evelyn. She's awesome, too."

After focusing her attention on meticulously lining up her tools on the granite countertop, she reached into her backpack for her notepad, casually asking, "Are you, um, planning to go to Zach's next weekend?"

"That's the plan, if my tutor will give me the day off," he said, nudging her in the arm.

"I think that can be arranged, especially after your fantastic B+ on the last science test."

"Thanks," he said sarcastically. "Anyway, with the regular season almost over, it will be nice to hang out and celebrate before the playoffs. You coming?"

Mia shrugged. "Probably. I'm just glad to have something to celebrate. If it wasn't for you, the team would still be on a losing streak."

"It's a team effort, Mia." Bryce reached into the large stainless refrigerator, pulling out a fresh carton of eggs.

"Yeah, right," she said with a snicker. "I love Zach to death, but there's no way he would've pulled off that second-quarter *Flea Flicker* play. As hard as his dad tried, Zach totally wasn't into being the quarterback."

Bryce's eyes grew bright as he almost dropped the eggs on the spotless floor. "You know that play?"

Mia let out a soft *snort*. "Of course. Who doesn't? Zach's dad made sure I knew all the cool trick plays."

Relaxing his elbows on the counter, his eyes turned soft. "Did you know his dad well?"

"Oh, yeah. He was the best. Taught me how to throw a spiral when I was a little kid. Believe me, my dad can make the best risotto or cannoli around, but he's completely clueless with a football. My mom was more the athlete, in cross-country and track."

Bryce grew quiet for a beat. "My mom was an athlete, too."

"Oh?" Mia replied. "What sport?"

"Softball," he mumbled. Turning away from her and the conversation, he changed the subject. "Um, aren't we supposed to preheat the oven or something?"

"Yeah. In a bit. But I want to show you what we're making."

Joining her at the counter, he peeked over her shoulder at her little notepad. "I thought we were making cannoli."

"We are. Just a sort-of variation," she said, pointing to her drawing. "Call it my 'good offense.'"

"Huh?" Bryce pushed her pad under to glow of the pedant lights, inspecting her detailed illustration. "Wow. That's cool. But what are they exactly?"

With her head high, Mia announced, "These"—she paused for effect—"are cannoli *cookies*."

Chapter 24

Mia was trembling with anticipation when she pulled the cookie "shells" from the oven. "So, next we let them cool and then add the filling to one side, topping it with the other. It's like a ... cannoli-sandwich-cookie-treat. Oh, and of course, the crowning touch is the perimeter of chopped pistachios."

"How's the filling going?" Bryce asked.

Mia dipped her pinkie into the bowl of creamy filling, then did the same with her dad's cannoli. She made a face, looking uncertain. "I don't know. I mean, it's okay. Just think there's something missing."

Bryce plunged a spoon into the bowl. "Tastes good to me. But we know I'm not the expert here." She heaved an exasperated sigh, aimlessly stirring her bowl of subpar filling. "Mia, it's not that bad. We can try again. Rome wasn't built in a day."

She glared at him from her mixing bowl. "Was that supposed to be an Italian reference? Because it was really bad."

He grinned sheepishly. "Kinda. Here's another one: how about we order a pizza while we wait for these to cool? Unlike you bakers, I can't live on sugar alone."

While Bryce called for the pizza, Mia started another bowl of filling, using a different combination of lemon, orange, and vanilla. Testing it again, she made a grimace, slamming the stainless bowl down on the counter with a loud *bang*. "Ahh!" she exclaimed, marching out of the kitchen.

"Yeah. Maybe you need a break," Bryce joked, stifling some laughter and joining her in the living room.

Mia ripped off her apron and collapsed into the plush leather sofa. Immediately, she was drawn to a framed family photograph sitting on the side table. Picking it up, she recognized a beaming Bryce modeling a Wellington football uniform in deep burgundy, the dazzling sun bouncing off his sparkling hazel eyes. Beside him stood his strait-laced dad and a beautiful woman with wavy brown hair, light eyes, and dimples. "She was so pretty," Mia said quietly as Bryce took a seat beside her.

"Yeah," he said softly.

"What was she like?" Mia found herself asking.

Bryce looked beyond her, the corners of his mouth slowly forming into a smile. "She was fun and carefree. We would toss this orange Nerf football around the apartment. Of course, she had a great softball arm, so she could really chuck a ball across the room. Drove my dad nuts."

"Do you still have it?"

"What? The football?" She nodded, and his smile turned playful. "I must have it, somewhere. Hold on." When he disappeared up the spiral staircase, Mia leapt off the sofa and returned to the kitchen. She finished the cannoli cookies, adding chilled filling from the fridge and rolling the edges in a pool of pistachios.

Mia was walking back into the living room when Bryce shot the orange, spongy football down the stairs toward her. She caught it with ease as he jumped down the final few steps. "Nice catch. Okay. Go long." Moving backward, he waved her farther into the room.

She hesitated while gripping the ball, her eyes skimming the fine artwork, expensive lamps, and ornate mirrors around her. "I don't know, Bryce. What if I break something?"

He shrugged. "Then, I'll tell Evelyn, and she'll replace it before my dad finds out."

"Why do I have a feeling you're telling me the honest truth?"

Shrugging again, he said, "Maybe Evelyn and I are tight, too." Mia beamed, crossing the length of the living room. She passed him the ball, and it sailed as light as air into Bryce's waiting hands.

Backing up even more and almost touching the balcony door, he chucked the ball across the space. As it landed in Mia's hands, she heard a door slam. Suddenly, a woman with short, light blonde hair emerged from the foyer. She was wearing a surprised, but pleasant, expression while holding a large pizza box. "Bryce? I caught the delivery guy downstairs." Her eyes homed in on Mia's hands. "Did I interrupt something?"

As Mia stood rigid, holding the football, Bryce moved forward, taking the pizza box. "Thanks for this. We were just having a bit of fun while we waited for dinner." Using the box, he pointed across the room. "Evelyn, this is Mia, my tutor." While he carried the pizza into the kitchen, Mia stood shocked, taking calming breaths to slow her erratic heart rate.

"Oh, yes. Tutor and baker." Evelyn offered her hand with a sincere smile. "So nice to meet you." When Mia took her hand, she added, "And you have quite the arm there."

Now relieved, Mia found her voice. "Thank you. It's great to meet you. And thanks for, uh, shopping."

Evelyn nodded, heading for the kitchen. "Of course. What exactly are you making?"

"Cannoli cookies," Bryce answered, opening the pizza box. "You hungry, Evelyn?"

"No, thank you. I already ate. But these cookies look delectable. Definitely save me one," she said with a wink. "If you two are all set, I'm going to get started on the laundry."

When she'd left down the long hallway, Mia whispered, "She does your laundry, too? Geez. I totally brought the wrong bags here." Bryce started laughing as he handed her a plate.

An hour later, Mia collected her backpack and the grocery bags, and Bryce walked her to the door. "You're sure you want to leave all these cookies here? It's more sugar than we can eat in a year."

"Well, the best way to hide the evidence is to eat it. Anyway, I made detailed notes on what did and didn't work, so feel free to share them with Evelyn or Sal." Adjusting one of the grocery bags, she spotted the orange football tucked inside and pulled it out. "What's this all about?"

"Guess you're hiding my evidence, too. Just keep it for . . . next time."

Mia carefully slipped the ball back into the bag and started for the door. She paused for a moment, then turned back. "Can I ask you a question?"

Bryce folded his arms over his chest. "I know I might regret this, but yes."

"Why'd you invite me here to bake?"

Giving her a lopsided grin, he relaxed against the door. "Because I know you need to keep this from your dad. And, well, I like it."

"The baking?" she asked, in disbelief. When he slowly nodded, Mia was thoughtful for a moment. "My answer is 'yes,' by the way." As he raised his eyebrows, she clarified, "Yes, I want to be friends."

Bryce opened the door with a face full of dimples and a wink. "Good, Mia. Because it looks like we already are."

Chapter 25

On Saturday afternoon, Mia was greeted by a set of adorable green eyes on the doorstep of Zach's cozy ranch. Her greeter adjusted his plastic knight's helmet, revealing a serious look. A lightsaber gripped in one hand, he draped his arms across the threshold and proudly proclaimed, "You *must* pay the toll!"

Bending down to meet his eyes, she mulled over his request. "Hmm. What's it gonna be today, Sir Eli?" She slowly opened the cardboard box in her hands, dramatically displaying its contents. "How about a cannoli cookie? It's a *thing* now, hopefully."

Nodding enthusiastically, he dropped his arms and took the largest cookie in the box. Without another word, he turned on his heel and flew into the house, running flat-out into his older brother. "Hey, bud. What do you have there?" Zach asked.

"Cannoli cookie from Queen Mia. She rules all," he said, sprinting off.

Zach smiled at his best friend as she deposited her windbreaker and bike helmet onto a bench near the front door, then crossed into the living room. "Seriously, Mia. You're his favorite person on the planet. I can't get him to call me King."

"Nah. It's the baked goods. Let's face it. By now, I probably reek of sugar. I like 'ruling all,' by the way. Not sure why the Queen has to pay a toll, though." She laughed and gave Zach a quick hug.

"Glad you made it. What are cannoli cookies? Those sound fab."

"It's our 'good offense,' but still a work in progress. Here—probably keep the rest away from Eli." Mia passed him the cardboard box. "And my dad wouldn't let me leave without bringing some sausage and peppers. You know, the norm." She loaded him down with a Pyrex dish, topped with a wrapped loaf of Italian bread.

They headed into the inviting kitchen, where Zach set everything down between dozens of soda bottles and chip bags. "Well, thank your dad, as always. My mom is gonna be thrilled. She has her hands full with work and Eli. Age four is not any easier than three, no matter what they say."

Mia lounged her elbows on the counter. "Sorry I've been so M.I.A. lately. Things are crazy at the bakery and school. Even had to stay late to help my dad fill a catering order today, thank goodness."

He gave her a sympathetic look. "Still bad, huh? At least you have some larger gigs, though, right?"

"Few and far between, unfortunately. Of course, it would help if my dad would get on social media like the rest of the world. Even our website is pathetic. I swear it's from before I was born!"

"Well, at least it exists. But I agree. It's kinda circa ten years ago." Grabbing a plastic cup, he filled it from the fridge's in-door ice maker and poured her a soda, sliding it across the counter.

"So, anyway, I'd be happy to come over to help babysit whenever you need. I know it's been a while, but I shouldn't be too out of practice. I mean, I *am still* the Queen, after all."

Zach emptied a Doritos bag into a large bowl. "Mia, you don't have to do that. You're so busy, you're barely getting sleep."

Sipping her soda and stealing a chip from the overflowing bowl, she said, "I'm not too busy for friends, Zach. Although, you're practically family by now. Speaking of which, where's your mom?"

"She's out back, manning the grill." Taking the bowl, he gestured toward the patio door. "We should head out, so I can relieve her from nonstop burger duty. Everyone's probably hounding her by now."

Mia hesitated. "Is, uh, Bryce here?"

"Wait. You guys aren't on the outs again, are you? I thought he said you hung out."

She gaped at him. "He said that?"

"Mia! You're finally here!" Harper exclaimed, strolling in from the backyard with Logan on her heels. She cut her eyes to the containers on the counter. "Are these the final product? Wow. Chloe's gonna be stoked."

Mia shook her head. "I wish. Something's off with the filling. Flavor's still not quite right."

Logan downed two cookies in succession, giving a thumbs-up. "Tastes amazing to me. Thanks, Mia." Lobbing another cookie into his mouth as he started for the door, he said, "Zach, the crew is getting restless out there. I don't think your mom could possibly flip fast enough."

Zach followed him, announcing, "Duty calls."

Before Harper could join them, Mia signaled her over to the corner of the kitchen. "Is Bryce out there?" she whispered anxiously.

Harper shot her a bemused side-glance. "Of course, he is, Mia. Just look for the guy surrounded by the cheerleaders and, well, Chloe."

"Why didn't she try out this year? She loves cheering, and she's been doing gymnastics ever since she could walk." Mia nervously peered around the corner, toward the door.

"I think she wanted a break before things got more serious. You know, JV versus varsity stuff. She still hangs out with everyone, though. Anyway, why are you avoiding Bryce?"

Blowing out a sigh, she threw up her hands. "Honestly. I don't know. Things are just *complicated*."

Harper studied her for a moment. "Yeah, well, maybe it's time you figured it out, boss." She grabbed Mia's arm and dragged her out the door.

When they entered the tree-lined backyard, packed with rowdy teenagers, Mia took a visual tour. Across the spacious lawn dotted with brownish-gold leaves, numerous circles of conversations surrounded a table brimming with snacks and refreshments. Like Harper had said, Bryce was easy to locate, dead center of a large group with his dimples in full force. He was clearly enjoying the attention as head cheerleader Abbie patted his arm while giggling just a bit too hard. On the patio, flames shot high into the air from the charcoal grill, where Zach and his mom took turns flipping juicy burgers atop an infinite number of buns. For a moment, Mia debated finding out what Abbie's hilarious conversation was all about but opted for the grill.

"Can I help, Lauryl?" Mia asked Zach's mom, whose face instantly lit up from behind the plume of smoke.

"Mia! How wonderful to see you! We've missed you." She beamed, dropping her spatula and pulling her into a warm embrace.

Just then, Eli ran out in full knight gear, his lightsaber waving high. "Time for battle!" he cheered, pulling his mom from Mia and the grill.

Laughing, Zach said, "I got this, Mom. Come on, Sir Eli. I'll find my lightsaber," scooping up his brother and heading for the house. Mia watched Lauryl Redding's green eyes lovingly follow her sons into the house.

"Lauryl, I'm sorry I haven't stopped by recently. I told Zach I could babysit anytime."

Zach's mom resumed flipping burgers, now looking a bit more relaxed. "Mia, you've helped plenty over the years. It's about time you focus on your amazing academics and leadership position. Your parents must be so proud." She passed her a plate with a piping-hot burger dripping gooey cheese and patted her on the back. "Zach's dad would've loved to see how far you've come."

Reluctantly taking the plate, Mia simply nodded as deep guilt rose to the surface. Lauryl continued serving one linebacker and one spunky cheerleader after another while Mia trudged over to the condiment table. She was adding ketchup and lettuce to her burger when Abbie ran up, gently tugging on her long ponytail. "Hey, girl. Haven't seen you around much. Guess running the ninth grade keeps you pretty busy, huh?"

Mia forked a tomato, placing it on top of her lettuce. "Yeah. Lots going on, I guess. At least the games have been good, right?"

"Well, thanks to our new star quarterback. He's even bringing out the best in Zach." Abbie's eyes glazed over the backyard and fell on the large group, including Bryce, enjoying snacks, burgers, and boisterous conversations. Inching closer to Mia, she lowered her voice. "So, guess you've been busy with tutoring, too?"

Grabbing a handful from the Ruffles bag, Mia shrugged. "Sure. But not for too much longer, I think."

Abbie's eyes grew as wide as saucers. "Why? You and Bryce not getting along?"

"Nah. I just think he's up to speed, is all. He's smart anyway, so it wasn't hard." Mia could hardly believe the words coming out of her mouth. *Wasn't hard? Really?* She bit into her burger while internally shaking her head.

As Abbie stepped even closer, she wound her golden blonde ringlets between her fingers and whispered casually, "So, are you and Bryce, um, a *thing*?"

Mia did a double take, almost choking on her next bite of burger. *Where did she get that idea? Chloe?* Taking a hard swallow, she answered an emphatic, "No. We're just friends. But, um, why do you ask?"

"I don't know," she said, giving a shrug. "Kinda the way he looks at you. Anyway, see if you can get Chloe on the squad next year. She's so much fun. Good seeing you!" Abbie squeezed her arm before returning to her circle.

As Mia questioned whether she could hold down the rest of her burger, Harper joined her, stealing one of her chips. "What was that all about? Abbie looked like she was sharing C.I.A. secrets with you."

Dropping the burger onto her plate, she answered flatly, "Nothing important. You want this?"

"No, thanks. Logan mentioned a potential game opportunity in a bit. Need to start practicing," she said with an energetic air kick.

Normally, a football scrimmage with her friends sounded like a blast, but Mia's mind was swimming between her concerns over Lauryl and now Bryce. Even the bakery seemed like a distant concern.

Harper ran off toward Logan, and Mia wandered over to pitch her unappetizing plate into the closest trash can. As she tossed in her napkin, a football flew her way. Looking up at the right moment, she caught it without much fanfare. Suddenly, she heard a familiar voice in the distance. "Great catch, as always." Lifting her curious gaze, Mia saw a set of hazel eyes approach with a mischievous grin and raised eyebrows. "So, you game?"

Chapter 26

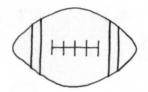

Crossing the arms of his navy and gold football hoodie, Bryce stood casually in the middle of Zach's backyard, sporting a pair of faded blue jeans and sneakers. His dark brown hair was a mass of messy waves, untidily held back by a pair of aviator sunglasses. With all traces of his pristine private school appearance gone, Mia almost didn't recognize him. If it wasn't for his impressive physique, dimples, and striking eyes, he almost blended in with his classmates.

"Well, Ms. DeSalvo?" He pocketed his glasses and combed his fingers through his sunlit hair.

But, before she could answer, Zach chimed in beside her. "Come on, Mia. You know you want to be our other quarterback."

She hesitated, her eyes shifting from the football to Bryce, giving her a once-over from a few yards away. "Unless. You're afraid you're gonna lose. To *me*," he teased, pushing up his sleeves.

Mia raised her narrowed gaze to fully meet his. "Not. A. Chance." Hurling the ball back, she grinned as it made a loud slapping sound against his palms.

"That's what I thought," he said, wringing out his hand with a full-on smile.

Zach, the natural captain, made a signal for everyone to huddle up. Mia was surprised to see Abbie drag Chloe into the group. "Do I *have* to?" she whined. "You can be on my team," Mia replied to her, giving Harper a look that said, *as long as she never gets the ball.*

Bryce threw Zach the football, giving him free rein to take over. "Okay. So, here are the rules. Wait. Where is everyone?" He peered over the huddle at most of the team and cheerleaders eagerly vying for the best seats on the grass. Sighing, he said, "Guess this is all of us. Everyone else just wants to be entertained."

Harper's eyes flicked from Mia to Bryce. "Yeah. I think we know why."

"Anyway," Zach continued. "It's two-hand touch, so *no* tackling. We'll do four chances to score, in lieu of downs. Punt off to start. And five-Mississippi blitz count."

"I don't even understand what the heck you just said, Zach," Chloe groaned.

"Chloe, just wait for me to throw the ball or rush, er, run," Mia translated.

"Exactly," Zach said. "And six points per touchdown." He dashed over to each side of his yard, placing two orange plastic cones for each goal line, to outline their "field." Jogging back to the huddle, he asked, "So, how do we feel about kicking?"

Logan and Harper exclaimed in unison, "Absolutely!"

"Okay, then. Good kick after touchdown earns an extra point. Any other questions before we pick teams?"

"Are we doing 'rough touch?'" Mia asked, crossing her arms.

"What does that mean?" Chloe asked, her voice filled with concern.

Zach answered, "Basically, you can shove to stop the play. Does everyone feel comfortable with that?"

"I'm game," Abbie said, resulting in Chloe shooting her a sneer and a hard punch in the arm.

Bryce's eyes fell on a defiant Mia. "Good with me."

"That depends," Logan answered with apprehension. "Can Harper and I just play kickers and punters?"

"Why?" Mia asked. "You're still taller and bigger than me."

"Yeah, well, you kinda have a dark side, Mia. No offense."

"Offense taken," she said, through clenched teeth as the huddle tried to stifle its laughter. Bryce could barely compose himself, almost doubling over.

"Okay. So, 'rough touch' to stop the play, but *nobody* should be on the ground." Zach slid a glance at Mia as she rolled her eyes. "Does that work for you, Logan?"

The kicker nodded, still looking uneasy.

Grabbing sets of practice jerseys, Zach handed gold to Mia and blue to Bryce. "Okay. Time to pick teams."

"Ladies, first," Bryce said sweetly to Mia.

"Fine. I'll take Harper," she said, her kicker skipping to her side.

"Logan," Bryce said.

"Zach," Mia said, and he happily pulled a gold jersey over his head.

With Abbie quietly pleading, Bryce chose her next.

"You're on my team," Mia said, signaling to a trembling Chloe, who reluctantly came forward for a jersey.

They continued to choose team members until each had six players, coaxing a few cheerleaders, who were about as disinterested as Chloe in actually playing. But the pull of being mere feet from their quarterback's famed biceps was enough to recruit.

Tossing a coin up into the air, Mia announced, "Heads!" right before it landed heads up on the grass. "Receive!"

Everyone clapped hands, and Mia's team lined up to receive Logan's kick. "Good luck," Bryce said to Mia, with a wink she swore looked sincere.

Expecting a skillful kick, Mia positioned herself on the far end of the yard. When the ball flew high into the sunny afternoon sky and across the length of their field, she caught it with ease. She swerved around Abbie and moved two-thirds of the way to the cones before Logan shoved her to stop the play.

"I kinda like this now. Good idea, Mia," he teased.

She glared at him. "Yeah. Watch out, Logan. Remember, you have to play offense, too." Mia smirked at the worried look on his face and waved her team in for a huddle. "Zach, go long," she whispered. "Let's try to get this one in the end zone and remind 'em who's boss."

"Confident and cocky," he said with an approving nod. "I like it."

After Harper's snap, while everyone counted Mississippis, Mia made eye contact with Zach. She launched a perfect spiral into the air that landed in his hands mid-run. He crossed the orange cones before Bryce could get even a few paces down the field. A short celebration ensued, with the rest of the backyard cheering, followed by a flawless kick by Harper. "7 to zip," Mia said proudly, sauntering by Bryce as he playfully bowed down.

Returning to the line of scrimmage, Mia was focused on Bryce during Harper's kick. Knowing his speed and propensity for easy rushing, she was surprised when he caught the snap and swiftly threw the ball to Logan. Mia charged for him, shoving Logan as he stepped into the imaginary red zone. "Nice catch," she grumbled.

"Thanks for not killing me," Logan teased, elbowing her.

The next play took only a split second. Bryce maneuvered around everyone—including a still disinterested Chloe, scarfing down a handful of chips and chatting with a couple of cheer girls—and rushed straight into the end zone. "Chloe! At least *pretend* you care," Mia moaned while Chloe shrugged between crunches. Logan easily kicked the ball straight through the orange cones, to tie it up at 7 to 7.

The plays continued in the same fashion until the score reached 21 to 21. As Mia gripped the ball, under the pressure of her five-count blitz, her eyes locked on Bryce. Faking a handoff to Zach, she rushed past Bryce at lightning speed. She started grinning, seeing a clear path, with nothing stopping her. That is, until Bryce caught up, shoving her only feet from the cones, sending her flying. "Sorry," he said, like a reflex, then added, "You okay?" He offered her a hand, which she immediately ignored.

Mia brushed some dirt and grass off her jersey as she scrambled upright. "Yeah. Just. Surprised," she answered breathlessly. "Didn't see you come up behind me."

"Yeah. You were pretty focused on your goal. Always be aware of what's going on behind you." Still bent at the waist, catching her breath, she internally rolled her eyes. "You sure you're all right?" he asked, patting her on the back.

She waved off his concerns, starting to walk away. "Bryce, I'm fine. I'm tougher than you think."

"Oh, I'm aware, Ms. DeSalvo—believe me," he mumbled, returning to the line of scrimmage.

When Mia passed Harper the ball on the fourth and final attempt, Bryce intercepted it and raced down the field for a touchdown. Her heart sank, watching the celebration on the other side of the field. "Sorry, Mia," Harper muttered.

"It's okay. Wasn't my best throw anyway."

Lining up for the kickoff, Bryce and Mia's eyes held for a beat as he mouthed, "Sorry," once again. She shook it off and focused on the snap and handoff to Harper, who gained a handful of yards until Logan carefully shoved her off the sidelines.

"Okay. My watch says 'one-minute warning,' so just a couple possessions to go," Zach announced. "Blue is up 28 to Gold's 21."

During the next play, Mia managed to rush Gold only a few yards before Abbie shoved her with a giggle. "Look who has the dark side now!" Mia shouted, caught off-guard.

With only seconds left in play, a frustrated Mia pulled her team aside for a huddle. "Zach, how about we give Bryce a taste of his own medicine? Maybe a little *trick play?*"

As Zach craned his neck over the huddle at their opposing quarterback, he looked skeptical. "I don't know, Mia. You sure Bryce isn't gonna recognize his own favorite play?"

Diverting her attention across the field, she smiled slyly. "There's no greater danger than underestimating your opponent, right? Let's see if Bryce remembers that."

"All right, Mia. It's risky, but you're the boss." Zach gave some quick instructions, and everyone clapped to break the huddle.

Giving Zach a look of intensity, Mia spun the ball on its laces and waited the whole five-count before handing it off to him. Then, as Bryce lunged toward him, Zach passed it back to Mia. She fired it straight at Chloe, waiting unpro-tected (for obvious reasons), smack-dab in the middle of the end zone.

"Yesss!" Chloe squealed when the picture-perfect pass landed in her hands. She spiked the ball on the ground, kick-ing up a few leaves in a cute victory dance, then accepted a high-five from Zach.

Chuckling to her very proud self, Mia had to admit Bryce looked pretty adorable, hands-on-hips, shaking his head in the middle of the field. He pushed out some air and raked his fingers through his disheveled waves as she mean-dered by. "Well played, Mia. Well played," he said, flashing a full-dimpled smile.

After another stellar kick by Harper, things were tied up 28-28. Zach's watch wound down, and he declared a draw, much to Mia's dismay.

As everyone shook hands to rousing applause by the rest of the backyard, Mia met up with an amused Bryce. "Are we still friends, Ms. DeSalvo, or are you gonna tackle me in science lab?"

"Sorry. Guess I'm a bit ..."

"Crazy?"

With crossed arms, Mia held her chin up high. "I was going to say *competitive*. Some might even say 'passionate.'"

"Yeah. I see that. Thanks for taking it out mostly on Logan and not me."

"Well, it wasn't intentional. He's just easier to catch. Next time," she said, lifting her shoulders in a shrug.

"I'll keep that in mind. Geez, you're something else, Mia DeSalvo."

Chapter 27

A few minutes later, Mia found herself clutching a lightsa-ber in an intense battle with Sir Eli in the kitchen. "How is the Queen even involved in this?" she called out in hysterics as Eli vigorously swept his lightsaber back and forth. "This has got to be some kind of coup attempt or something!"

"A what?" he asked, still focused on his lightsaber.

Looking past Eli, Mia noticed Bryce, standing alone in front of a tall bookshelf in the living room. "I surrender," she proclaimed, holding up her hands as Eli giggled and jumped up and down in victory. She cut her eyes back at Bryce and said softly, "Eli, I think there are a few cannoli cookies left. Tell Zach you earned one from battle, okay?"

"Thanks, Queen Mia," he hollered, running out the back door.

Leaning the lightsaber against the wall, Mia padded into the quiet living room. When she got closer, she saw Bryce's eyes moving between two photographs: one with Zach and his dad, both in uniform (one football, one Army), and a younger photo of Zach's dad, holding a football while sporting a blue uniform with a gold number 5.

"That's Zach's favorite with his dad," Mia said, pointing to the photo of both father and son in uniform. "It was taken shortly before he passed away. You know, he played for West Point after he won GW the State Championship."

"Yeah. Coach has us watching his films. He was amazing. It was Zach's idea for me to wear his number."

She smiled. "I can believe it. It's been a while since anyone could do it justice."

"Not sure I'm the right person for it," he said flatly, his gaze landing on a folded American flag, displayed in a triangular case on the top shelf.

"Seems like yesterday that the officers showed up," she said in a hushed tone, gesturing to the front door.

Bryce tore his eyes from the white five-pointed stars amid Old Glory Blue and gave her a look of disbelief. "You mean, *you* were *here*?"

"Yeah. Zach and I were playing catch out back. It was really … tough." Mia's voice shook a bit. She swallowed a burning lump in her throat, shrugging it off. "But I'm glad I was here. When someone loses someone, it's important to let them know you're there, if and when they need you."

He continued to stare at her, then was contemplative. "That's how you understand," he muttered to himself.

"Understand?" she said softly.

Directing his attention back to the photographs, Bryce's tone again turned cool. "You know, I never even cried. My dad didn't either. Don't you think that's wrong?"

Mia took a moment to absorb his intimate confession. "Not really, Bryce," she said softly. "My mom says people process grief differently. I don't think there's a *right* or a *wrong.*"

Narrowing his eyes at her, he snapped, "There should be. A person's life is too important to just forget."

Taken aback by his candid anger, she hesitated, then said, "It's up to us, those left behind, to remember. That's what I hope I'm doing every time I bake something from Nonna Antoinette. It's like the bakery is keeping her memory and her legacy alive. And it's what you do when you proudly wear Captain Redding's number 5."

Bryce nodded, then took in a shaky breath. "So, what do I do for my mom, then?"

Chapter 28

Bryce's question continued to haunt Mia throughout the weekend. She wanted to come up with some magical answer to his profound question. But no matter how hard she tried, nothing of any consequence seemed to surface.

With the first round of playoff games happening on Saturday, the school atmosphere was electric. It had been a while since GW High's Eagles could celebrate a winning football season and potential bid to the State Championship Final. Mia and the rest of the student council declared it "Spirit Week," with everyone displaying plenty of navy-blue and gold for the special occasion.

By the time Mia made her way into science class on Friday, the whole room felt on edge, the air practically tingling with anticipation for the next day's game. So, she was relieved to see their star quarterback in a relaxed and upbeat mood. "Morning, Bryce," she said cheerfully, checking out his immaculate practice jersey that he casually sported with a pair of dark jeans. "Evelyn did a great job with your uniform."

"Thanks," he said, showing off his full dimples. "Your hair looks nice."

She smoothed out her long locks, pushed back by a blue and gold headband. Feeling her face flush, she quickly changed the subject. "Um, did Zach tell you about tomorrow night, at the bakery?"

"Yeah. Hopefully, we'll have something to celebrate, right?"

"Well, if not, we can drown our sorrows in carbs and sugar. It's right after the game, if you need to ask your dad. Is he, um, coming?"

Bryce shook his head, his dimples fading. "Nah, probably not. Gotta work. Think he has a deadline or something."

Mia leaned over the lab table with interest. "What does he do exactly?"

"He's an architect," he muttered as his eyes traveled to his textbook.

"Oh. That sounds cool," she said, but Bryce simply shrugged. Trying to elevate his now sullen mood, she added, "I know I've only met him once, but he seemed nice. Maybe I could bring dinner to your place or something? Get to know him better?"

He looked up from his book, incredulous. "You'd want to do that?" She nodded, and he shook his head to himself. "Wow. You really are something else, Mia."

"Whenever you say that, Bryce, it sounds like a bad thing." She crossed her arms and slumped into her seat.

"Trust me, it's not."

Meanwhile, Ms. Marsh initiated her chalk clicking, focused on "The Importance of the Periodic Table." When

Mia continued to sulk, Bryce gave her a wink and a playful nudge. Smiling in return, she pulled out her notebook and a pencil from her backpack. As she set it on the ground, she managed to catch Chloe behind her, so engrossed in their every move all that was missing was a box of popcorn. Mia sank even deeper into her seat, stealing a glance at her lab partner, dutifully taking notes.

When the bell finally ended Ms. Marsh's epic lesson, the exhausted class was grateful for the reprieve. As Bryce packed up his messenger bag, he turned to Mia. "So, I guess I'll see you at the game and then after, right?"

"Sure. Sounds good." The second he disappeared out the door, Mia faced Chloe, who was clearly lingering a little too long by her lab station. "What the heck were all those faces about?" she hissed.

Chloe feigned innocence. "Nothing." But apparently, Mia had *unconvinced* written all over her face. "Fine. Grab Harper, and we'll meet by the vending machines at lunch."

"Huh?" she asked as Chloe headed for the door without further explanation.

When Mia arrived at their vending machine rendezvous a few hours later, Harper was hands-on-hips annoyed, her eyes darting across the packed cafeteria.

"Any idea what this is all about?" Mia asked, pulling a paper bag and a bottle of water from her backpack.

"No clue. But I didn't have any breakfast, so this better be quick." Rising onto her toes, Harper scanned the room, then moaned, "Seriously, Chloe? You have got to be kidding me," dropping her head in her hand.

"What?" Mia snagged a bite from her PBJ and shifted her gaze around the lunch chaos.

"She's in the Boar's Head line. We're gonna be waiting here forever!"

Stopping mid-bite, Mia gave her unappealing homemade sandwich a second glance. With a grimace, she deposited it back into her bag. "She sure as heck better share then."

Harper impatiently tapped the toe of her sneaker on the vinyl tile. "Anyway, while we're *waiting*, I wanted to let you know the chocolate bar sales are doing pretty well."

"Great. Thanks for taking care of all these details. I knew you'd be perfect as committee chair." Mia scrunched up her nose and gave her head a shake. "Wait. *Pretty* well?"

"Yeah. I mean, they're decent, but we have this to compete with." Harper kicked one of the packed vending machines behind her. "But the football concessions should bring in a good amount. Thank goodness for a winning team and an extended season."

Mia nodded apprehensively. "Still not enough, though. I need to come up with a big event, and fast. The food bank could really use the money to help get through the winter."

"True. We can brainstorm this weekend, after the game. I know you'll think of something, boss. You always do." She patted Mia on the back as Chloe approached, balancing a tray of turkey and provolone on Italian bread amid a tall pile of chips and a steaming slice of pepperoni pizza.

"Here," Chloe said, handing the pizza to Harper, who instantly scarfed down a huge bite of cheesy goodness.

Trying to keep from drooling, Mia turned her attention away from the enticing tray. "So, what's with the under-cover meeting?"

Chloe balanced the tray against her hip. "Well, Mia. Why don't *you* tell us?"

"Huh? I have an epically disappointing lunch to finish. Could we cut the cryptic?"

Rolling her eyes, Chloe turned to Harper. "Well, our friend here appears to be holding out on us, regarding a certain adorable quarterback." When Mia remained confused, she continued, "Come on, Mia. I heard you and Bryce talking about this weekend. Meeting up. At the game. *And after?* You're planning a *date.*"

Mia stared with open-mouthed astonishment at her ridiculous suggestion while Harper's eyes widened. Shaking her head, she said, "Chloe! We're *friends*—just *friends*. Argh..." throwing up her hands. Then, starting to walk away, she added, "If you'll excuse me, I need to attend to that disappointing lunch."

"Hold on! Not so fast!" Harper tugged Mia back by the hood of her sweatshirt with her pizza-free hand. "I'm intrigued. Seriously, Mia. Spill."

Pivoting back, she groaned, "There's *nothing* to spill. He's coming to the bakery after the game, like everyone else we invited."

Harper looked thoughtful, taking another bite of pizza. "But you guys *do* hang out a lot."

"And you gotta admit he's hot and a sweetheart," Chloe added in a dreamy voice.

Mia let out an exasperated sigh. "Yes. Anyone with eyes can see he's good-looking. He's nice and smart. And yes, I like hanging out with him."

"And you gotta see it, right, Mia?" Harper asked.

"See what, exactly?"

Harper leaned close and whispered, "The way he looks at you," as Chloe sneaked a bite of her sandwich, looking captivated.

Mia was taken aback, having heard the same words from Abbie. Was she missing something? As she mentally pieced together the last several weeks of her life, she was starting to doubt her own instincts. "Maybe that's just how he looks at a good friend," she said quietly. "Right?"

She remained lost in her own thoughts as Chloe picked up the other half of her turkey and provolone, handing it over. "Here—looks like you're gonna need your strength to figure this out." Mia accepted the sandwich, now with more on her mind than she knew what to do with.

Chapter 29

The next night, when the massive crowd of blue and gold burst through the bakery door, sheer euphoria was felt by all. Thanks to an amazing quarterback and his equally impressive running back, the Eagles' place in the semifinals was secure.

As Mia approached a cheery Zach and his brother, sharing a table and some cannoli in a peaceful corner, she had to admit there *was* something to the thought that Bryce seemed to bring out the best in Zach. "Great night, huh?" she asked, sliding a chair over to join them.

Zach looked up with bright eyes and a wide grin. "Yeah. Tonight was pretty awesome. Can't remember the last time I had so much fun, especially on the field." He cut up a piece of cannoli for Eli, who was pleasantly covered in pistachios from head to toe.

Mia knew exactly when he'd seemed so happy—two years ago. "Well, your last catch in the end zone was pretty perfect. Your mom was so proud; she was beaming."

He laughed, offering his brother the last bite. "It helps to trust the guy throwing the ball. And, speaking of beaming, you seem especially happy these days."

"Oh? I figured I was a ball of nerves, between the fund-raising mess and the bakery."

"Nah. You're working all that out, Mia. I mean, *other* stuff." He pointed his chin in the direction of Bryce, encircled by Chloe, Abbie, and the rest of the cheerleaders.

She groaned. "Oh, no. Not you too!"

"What? You and Bryce are getting close, right? It helps to have a good friend around when you're dealing with the tough stuff."

Relief washed over Mia. Leave it to Zach to understand friendship better than anyone. "I guess we've had some decent chats."

Zach considered her comment for a moment. "Well, anyway, I'd better get this little guy home before he literally eats you out of house and bakery," he said, motioning to his over-sugared brother. "Thanks for organizing this. Hopefully, we can keep the momentum going for two more games." He stood and hugged her goodbye.

Eli grabbed his lightsaber, then gave her a tight squeeze. "Thanks, Queen Mia." Zach dragged him away with an eye roll, still removing pistachios from his hair.

Moving from the peaceful corner into the bustle of the rowdy bakery, Mia shifted her attention toward Bryce and his entourage. As she approached the group, hoping to join, suddenly she froze. From the edge of the shadows, her eyes were fixed on Chloe, who was also beaming—nonstop at Bryce. A sick feeling churned in Mia's stomach, knowing she had seen that look before, on Abbie in Zach's backyard. Perhaps Chloe's lunchtime inquisition wasn't so innocent after all.

Until she knew the real scoop, her plan was to keep her distance, at least for the night. When Bryce spotted her, she did an about-face. "Hey, Mia. Logan and I were bouncing around fundraising ideas," Harper said, waving her over. Mia nodded along but, all the while, kept Chloe and Bryce in the corner of her eye.

An hour later, only a few stragglers remained. Mia was preoccupied with her thoughts and cleaning the long marble counter when Bryce abruptly walked up in a jovial mood. "Hey! Need any help?"

Taken by surprise, she stumbled through a horrible, "Um, no thanks. I, um, got it," as she mindlessly continued to scrub the same spot.

"It's no problem. My dad's working late anyway, so I don't have to rush home." Mia focused on her mundane task, in hopes of avoiding eye contact. Looking amused, Bryce rested the elbows of his navy Henley on the counter. "I think you missed a spot," he teased. "I mean, you haven't *quite* scrubbed off the finish." She lifted her gaze only long enough to shoot him a smirk, then returned to her aggressive scrubbing. "Geez. If I didn't know any better, I'd say you were trying to avoid me."

Sighing, she pushed her rag to the side and started collecting dirty dishes from the tables. "I have a lot on my mind, is all."

"Anything you want to share?" he asked, following her.

Mia shook her head, placing dishes into a bin. "That's not usually how I work through stuff."

"Okay. How then?" He scooped up the last of the dishes and carried the bin to the counter for her.

Even though she wasn't sure why he even cared, she answered, "Usually, when I have something on my mind, I bake."

Bryce took in the empty room, watching the last of their classmates thank Mia and exit out the door. "Okay, then. Let's do it."

"Um, what?" She trudged to the door and threw the lock.

"Let's bake."

Mia glanced at the locked door, now wishing to be on the other side of it. "I don't know," she said, returning to the counter.

Bryce lounged against it, holding his ground. "Why? Is your dad around?"

She focused past him, confirming the espresso machine was turned off. "No. My mom said earlier he was fast asleep in his recliner."

"Okay. Then, why not? You know how I work through stuff, obviously."

Knowing he was referring to the infamous journal, Mia threw up her hands and relinquished her clean-up. "Fine, Bryce. But *you're* gonna help."

Chapter 30

With an impressive display of dimples, Bryce followed Mia into the kitchen, where she immediately draped an apron over his head. "Since you clearly have a thing against flour," she teased, tying it snugly around his waist. Their eyes held as she caught the blue reflection of the apron against his hazel gaze.

"It's growing on me," he teased back with a wink.

Spinning away from him, Mia rolled her eyes, pulling her own apron over her head. She headed to her cobalt KitchenAid mixer and picked it up with a *grunt*. Bryce sighed and scooped up one side, helping her carry the mixer to the stainless counter. "Thanks," she mumbled, running to preheat the oven.

Mia was fetching butter and eggs from the fridge when Bryce took a long look around the kitchen. "Why use this mixer when you have those big commercial ones?"

"My parents gave it to me last Christmas. They don't like me using the heavier equipment all the time."

"Well, you're probably the only baker in town with a mixer that matches her eyes."

"Oh. I didn't think about that. Honestly, it's my favorite color."

Bryce smiled with a glint in his eyes. "Makes complete sense to me." Mia tried to rub off the blush forming on her cheeks.

Shaking off his comment, she focused on measuring sugar in a stainless cup. While bending over the counter, her long locks fell over her shoulders, obscuring her view. "Geez. Every time," she grumbled, abruptly dropping the cup with a hair flip. When Mia searched her apron pockets and came up empty, she sighed. Bryce appeared fascinated as she turned and rose onto her toes. She yanked down a large spool of red and white baker's twine from an upper shelf and snipped off a few inches. Then, she collected her thick locks and tied them up with a bow. "Much better."

She added both white and brown sugar and a couple tablespoons of butter to the mixer while Bryce stood, smiling and attentive, beside her. "What are we making anyway?"

"Pistachio biscotti. I'm sure your mom would've like them." Mia pointed to the mixer as she carefully watched it spin to a smooth consistency. "I usually add a bit of butter and oil to the recipe. It's not as authentic but keeps you from breaking your teeth on the dough."

Bryce laughed and nodded his agreement.

When Mia added the eggs and other wet ingredients, Bryce inched even closer. His warmth radiated through her, making her skin tingle. Hoping for a distraction, she said, "So, why football? I mean, you're great, so you must've been playing for a while, right?"

"Thanks. Actually, it was my mom's idea when I was little. I guess I was one of those kids who couldn't sit still. So, she had to find some way to occupy my energy."

Mia pulled the large container of flour toward them and cracked it open, sending a small puff of fine powder into the air. Measuring out the flour, suddenly she went rigid. Checking her small notepad, she grimaced and scratched her head. "What the heck? How did I not write that down?"

"What's wrong?"

"Like a dummy, I forgot how much flour to use. I've been experimenting so much lately my brain is fried."

As her eyes slowly moved to the corner of the kitchen, Bryce backed away. "I get it, Mia. Go ahead. Look it up." Putting his hands up, he started to turn around.

Biting her nails anxiously, Mia blew out a sigh and relented. "Wait, Bryce!" He stopped and turned back to face her. "You can stay. It's fine."

"You sure?"

"Yeah. Come on." She waved him over to the tall shelves in the corner, where she placed a step stool.

Bryce's eyes followed her as she climbed the stool, balanced on her tiptoes, and leaned over the top step. "Be careful," he warned.

Mia bit her bottom lip, leaning in even farther. "Wow. This is jammed in more than usual. I think there is something else back here." She furrowed her brows until she finally clasped the spine of the book, letting out a shaky exhale. With one great yank, she lost her balance and was propelled backward. Tripping on her own two feet on the way down, she missed a step and went airborne. Bryce's dexterity was sharply tested, catching her just before she landed on the floor.

"Are you okay?" he asked breathlessly.

Still clutching the book, Mia burst into a fit of giggles. "Yeah. I'm fine, thanks. At least it wasn't flour, this time. You're lucky."

Bryce stared at her with wide eyes and helped her stand. "Geez, Mia. You do that all the time? You could've broken your neck!"

"Well, if that does happen, please make sure to put the book back before you call the ambulance. I'm dead serious, by the way."

"That's what I'm worried about." He gripped his chest, trying to catch his breath. "You totally freaked me out."

"Sorry. Thanks for the catch, though," she said, already thumbing through the book.

"Hey! This is cool." Bryce reached for the ratty football on the shelf, spinning it in his palm. "Strange place for a football, though," he joked.

Placing the recipe book on the counter, Mia's face turned serious. She swallowed a painful lump and stared down at her hands. "Actually. It's, um, Zach's dad's old ball. He, uh, gave it to me before his last deployment."

Bryce immediately went still, carefully offering it to her. "I'm so sorry, Mia. I didn't know," he said softly.

She smiled, gently setting it back on the shelf with a light pat. "That's okay. It's meant to be played with. I keep it here as a happy reminder."

"Happy?"

"Yeah. Some of my happiest childhood memories are here in this kitchen with the recipe book and that football. Made sense to keep them together."

Bryce's mouth slowly curved at the corners. "That *does* make sense."

Mia scooped up the recipe book, finding the correct page. "Yup. What I thought." After she slowly added the flour to the mixer with the other dry ingredients, including the toasted pistachios, she dropped the sticky dough onto the floured countertop, separating it into two sections. "Now, for the fun part. Is Mr. Chadwick Academy ready to get his hands messy?"

Rolling up his sleeves, he reached in without hesitation and grabbed one mound of dough. "You mean, *former* Chadwick Academy."

Mia demonstrated how to form a log with the dough, placing it on one side of the pan. Bryce then mimicked her movements, setting his version beside hers with his head high. "Excellent," she proclaimed. "Not bad for a boarding school guy." She playfully flicked bits of flour at his apron on her way to the oven, then set the timer.

"Former," he reiterated, shaking his floury hands at her, then heading to the sink for a quick rinse.

As Mia focused on the biscotti dough through the oven's glass door, she casually said, "Actually, that reminds me, Bryce. I was still wondering about something."

"Let me take a wild guess. Boarding school, right?" he called out from the sink.

Her eyes remained glued on the door as she shrugged. "Maybe."

"Mia, seriously?" He folded his arms over his apron as he met her by the oven.

Turning to face him, she nudged him with her elbow. "Come on, Bryce. You know where my great-great-grandmother's prized recipes are hidden. You gotta give me something. And Zach would agree." When he looked confused, she said, "Never mind. So, you were helping Sebastian, right?"

Burying his head in his now clean hands, he massaged his forehead. "Yes, Mia."

"Why?"

"Okay. You win, Mia DeSalvo!" Throwing up his hands, he collapsed onto one of the stools, and Mia followed. With a deep inhale, he started, "Sebastian and I were friends and teammates at Wellington. He's a decent guy and used to be a fantastic running back, like Zach. But he had a habit of getting into trouble, constantly. Like, he'd goof off and miss practice, which got him kicked off the team. Then, he stopped studying, and his grades took a nosedive. And you know what usually happens when you have too much free time on your hands ..."

"He got into more trouble?" she asked, fully immersed in his story but with one eye still watching the oven.

"Yep. His parents were sick of his antics and thought he needed around-the-clock supervision. So, off to Chadwick, he went. The thing was, he actually liked it. See, his home life was not the best. Sebastian's dad drank a lot and took it out on him. And his mom kinda didn't stop it."

Leaning on her elbows, Mia frowned. "That's sad."

"I know. So, whenever he had trouble with his school-work, I would help him out. You know, like you helped me."

She sat up, her posture stiffening. "Not exactly, Bryce. You didn't really need a tutor. I just caught you up a few chapters."

To her surprise, Bryce shot to his feet and abruptly left the kitchen for the bakery. When he returned with his puffer jacket, he pulled out two papers. "I wanted to show these to you. Another reason to celebrate." Her blue eyes sparkled seeing one large, red A on his latest algebra test, followed by another large, red A on his science test. "Mia, you're responsible for this. You taught me all those great tips. Math and science have never been my best subjects. Honestly, you're a great teacher."

As her gaze remained fixed on the papers, part of Mia was elated, while another felt her heart sink. With Bryce now "up to speed," was this the end of them hanging out together? When she lifted her eyes, her smile was sincere. "It was my pleasure."

"Not at first, though, right?" he teased, and she sheepishly nodded. "So, anyway, I would help Sebastian like you helped me, especially with his English papers. When I joined him at Chadwick this fall, he was stoked. But eventually, he started goofing off, again. No matter how hard I tried, he was already failing most of his classes. So, we decided to make a pact."

"You'd help him out?" she asked, once again riveted by his story.

"Actually, we were helping each other out. He needed the test answers to pass and stay at Chadwick and, if we managed to get caught, I'd happily take full responsibility."

Mia's jaw dropped. "Wait. You got caught *on purpose?*"

"Well, not 'on purpose.' But if someone had to take the fall and get expelled, I was it." When she gave him a blank expression, he clarified, "Mia, I hated even a few weeks of boarding school. It sucked being away from home, and I missed my football friends at Wellington. So, when my teacher asked who took the answers, I confessed. Sebastian couldn't get kicked out, but I could."

Mia rubbed her temple, clearing the cobwebs as she slowly took in Bryce's revelations. "But did you even *take* the answers?"

"Nah. I was just the lookout. It was all Sebastian. He stole the keys, broke in, took photos of the answers, and then locked them back up. We were too dumb to realize our teacher was grabbing a quick cup of coffee and easily caught me hanging out by the door."

"Wait a second, Bryce. Did Sebastian *use* the answers he found?"

"Probably. I don't know. I was too busy getting chewed out in the headmaster's office to find out. But, between us, he didn't have many scruples, unfortunately."

"But what about Wellington? Why didn't you go back there?"

Bryce shrugged. "Just the price I had to pay for a not-well-thought-out plan. When the Wellington trustees heard about my stunt, it was goodbye football and everything else."

Mia was stunned. "Wait. You ended up at GW because Wellington didn't want you back?"

"Yup." His shoulders lifted into another shrug. "It was worth it, though, to help Sebastian. He caused problems, sure. But he still didn't deserve the stuff at home. My life is a piece of cake compared to his."

With Mia's mind now spinning, she almost fell off her stool in surprise when the *beep* of a timer filled the space. She trudged to the oven in a haze, pulling the pan out. "Um. We just have to let the dough cool, then slice them at an angle and bake them a bit more." She was feeling light-headed, her voice sounding somewhere far off in the distance.

"You okay?" Bryce asked, stepping close and searching her eyes. "You don't think *less* of me now, do you?"

Mia held his intense gaze for several moments. "No, Bryce. I think even *more* of you now, if that's even possible."

Chapter 31

These look fantastic!" Mia said, assessing the twice-baked results on the pan a little while later. "Not bad for a newbie baker." She jabbed Bryce, who lit up the room with his adorable dimples.

"They smell amazing," he said, inhaling the pan's scrumptious aroma. "But how'd you know they were done before the timer went off?"

"Ah, that's easy. By that amazing smell. If they smell done, they're done."

Unable to contain his excitement, Bryce eagerly snatched a piping-hot cookie. Mia giggled as he juggled it in his hands a few times before blowing on it. "So, from one baker to another, why do you love it so much?"

She was pensive for a moment, taking a cookie from the pan. "Well, I grew up with it, of course. But I guess it's like solving a problem, like math and science, but still allows you to be creative. I mean, you have a formula, but there are so many possibilities. And the bakery is a way to share what I create."

"It keeps you busy, though. Must be hard finding time for school and stuff like class council."

"Yeah. All that stuff matters to me, too. Honestly, my mind has been preoccupied with this fundraising thing for the food bank. If we want to reach our goal, we need something bigger than a few lame candy bar sales."

"Mind if I ask why the food bank is so important? I mean, I know *why*, but why to *you*?" he asked, nibbling on his cookie.

"The food bank is awesome. It has helped so many of our customers and ... friends. It runs the local food pantries and soup kitchens, where we donate our extra baked goods. They're always appreciative of even one loaf of bread. Unfortunately, with us not doing as well, it's harder to find extras to donate." She gave her head a shake and pushed out a frustrated sigh. "Yeah. The bakery problem is a whole other issue on my mind. I just need to get my dad on board for some real changes. Don't even get me started on our ancient website."

Bryce seemed deep in thought while they enjoyed their crispy biscotti. They were cleaning the counter and collecting the dishes when he perked up brightly, as if a light bulb had clicked on overhead. "Mia, what if you could do both, at once?"

"Both?"

"Yeah. Help the food bank *and* get your dad's attention?

Her interest piqued, she dropped her rag, homing in on Bryce. "Okay. I'm listening."

"Well, how about a bake sale?"

Mia's face fell as her eyes filled with uncertainty. "I don't know, Bryce. Me selling cookies in the hallway between classes not only sounds sad but pathetic. Plus, everyone knows I pass them out for free."

"What if it was a big deal? Invite other bakeries and local food businesses. We could line up dozens of tables in the football stadium. Take advantage of the momentum from the winning season. You know, make it a real event."

Nodding, she started to picture it in her head. "While I'm not thrilled about inviting Urban Coffee to anything, their customer base could bring in some real cash."

"Yeah. And, this way, you get people trying your new recipes. Let them see you're better than Urban Coffee. Better yet, Mia, let your *dad* see how much better your stuff sells."

A massive grin stretched across her face. "Bryce, you're brilliant. This could work. And, best of all, we could make some real money for the food bank."

He flashed a proud smile. "Not so bad for a dumb jock, right?"

"You are far from that. You've been doing an amazing job in science and math. Not to mention, you're a brilliant quarterback. It's why we're in the playoffs."

Bryce's cheeks turned rosy. "Thanks. And you are a brilliant baker," he said, snagging another cookie.

"Thanks. I've got biscotti down. If only I could figure out the cannoli."

Several biscotti cookies later, they were finishing tidying up the kitchen when Bryce said, "You know. I've created a few websites if you need some help updating yours."

"You'd do that?" she asked, sliding the clean sheet pan back on a shelf.

"Of course. I like doing it, so it's no big deal."

"Awesome," Mia said, returning her apron to its hook. Suddenly, her eyes jumped to the creaking ceiling above. "We'd better finish up here, in case my dad wakes up." Then, she noticed the only remaining item on the counter: the recipe book. "Shoot. I forgot."

Cradling the heirloom, she started toward the shelf, but Bryce gently tugged her back by her ponytail. "No way, Mia. Let me do it."

"Fine," she said, but hesitated before handing him the book. "Please be careful. It's very old and delicate. And I don't want to be called out for harming our 'star quarterback.'"

"Thanks for your concern," he said sarcastically, mounting the precarious step stool. He gingerly slid the book back in place, then stopped. "Mia, you're right; there's something else back here." Digging farther into the shelf with his long arms, Bryce's face showed concentration, followed by triumph. "Got it!" he declared victoriously. When he pulled his hand from the depths of the shelf, he revealed a small amber bottle. "What the heck?"

Passing it to Mia, he watched her examine every detail of the bottle. When she unscrewed the top, releasing the fragrance, she gasped. "No way! It couldn't be!" She ran out of the kitchen at lightning speed while Bryce stood, perplexed.

Mia returned a split second later with one stray cannoli from the party. "Thank goodness I hid this one from Eli. My dad made it just this morning." She took another quick sniff from the amber bottle, followed by a spoonful of cannoli filling." With a glowing smile, she handed both the bottle and spoon to Bryce. "Okay. You try," she proclaimed proudly.

As instructed, he smelled the bottle, then tasted the cannoli. Looking at Mia, his face confirmed her suspicion. "I can't believe it."

"Yup. It was here the whole time. Literally, right under our noses."

Holding the bottle up to the light, Bryce stared at it with wide eyes. "*This* is the secret ingredient?"

"Yup," Mia said. "The right combination of floral, citrus, and vanilla: *Fiori di Sicilia*."

Chapter 32

After a successful class council meeting, Harper high-fived Mia in front of Ms. Marsh's science class the next Monday. Mia was so excited, she sprinted through the doorway to share the news with Bryce. But as she approached her lab station, she quickly noticed him immersed in an animated exchange with Chloe behind him, and her excitement faded. When Bryce looked up and spotted her, the conversation ended abruptly. "Morning, Mia," he said, his grin widening.

"Hey, Mia," Chloe said curtly, then resumed chatting with the group of cheerleaders around her.

As Mia sank deeply into her seat, so did her mood.

"Everything okay, or just the Monday blues?" he asked with sympathetic eyes.

She shrugged. "It's okay. Was gonna tell you I brought up your idea with the class council this morning, and we are a go for the bake sale."

"Awesome!" he exclaimed, offering Mia a high-five that she slapped with only slight interest. He studied her more closely. "That *is* awesome, right?"

"Yeah. Just a lot of work to do in the next couple of weeks. Harper's handling the local business connections, but it's now hitting me how much organizing and baking I'm gonna have to do in a short time."

"I could help," he said, pulling his books from his messenger bag.

"Thanks for the offer, Bryce, but you should be focused on the last two games of the season, especially this Saturday's semifinal. I'll think of something, I guess, even if it means no sleep for a while." She let out a *groan*, dropping her head onto the lab table.

Leaning closer, he said, "I had fun after the party on Saturday, so I'm always game."

"Well, we could still do that dinner thing at your place." She reached into her backpack, digging out her notebook. Returning her bag to the floor, she noticed Chloe taking in every word, once again. When Mia flashed her a smile, Chloe's lips curved only slightly as she quickly shifted her eyes down to the lab table. Mia spun back around and focused on the chalkboard, deciding to keep her mouth shut for the rest of the hour.

After a yawn-inducing lesson, highlighting the nuances of fossils, Mia lifted her stiff neck from her notebook and caught only Chloe's back heading out at the first sound of the bell. Slinging her backpack over her shoulder, she turned to Bryce. "Let me know when you are free for that dinner."

"You were serious? You actually want to have dinner with me and my dad?" he asked incredulously, loading up his bag.

Rushing for the door, Mia forced herself to stay fixed on a disappearing Chloe. "Of course. I make a mean lasagna."

Bryce stared at her, dumbstruck, as she hightailed it out the door at track star speed.

"Chloe!" Mia yelled out in the crowded hallway. After weaving her way around the long train of students, she finally caught up with her friend at her locker. "Hey," she said breathlessly, practically doubled over. "Haven't seen you much lately."

Chloe looked up from her book bag, pushing up her glasses. "Sorry. Been busy with the magazine. Deadlines are coming up."

"Actually. I was hoping to talk to you about that. Do you still have those advertising flyers, asking for submissions?"

"Sure." Rummaging through her book bag, she pulled out a bright blue sheet of paper. "You want to write something for the literary magazine?" she asked, with a curious look.

Mia shook her head. "Not quite. We both know that would be a horrible idea. Just a thought for someone else. But the deadline is soon, right?"

Chloe emptied the contents of her bag into her locker with a flourish. "Yeah. I can only wait like another week or so. Gotta get the stuff off to the printer. All the fun tasks go to the freshmen editors." She slammed her locker with an eye roll. "But at least it's hardcover this time, so it's pretty exciting."

"Definitely," Mia said enthusiastically, shoving the flyer into her backpack. Seeing Chloe eager to leave, her heart started to sink. "Listen. You think you and Harper might want to come over next weekend for a girls' night sleepover? Maybe bake a bit?" She held her breath as her stomach twisted into a tight knot.

With a jarring *chime*, Chloe's attention abruptly shifted to her cell phone. Her grin stretched wide as she started down the hallway. "Uh, yeah. A sleepover sounds good," she answered back, her eyes never leaving her screen. "See you around." Mia watched her rush off and couldn't help but notice the distance increasing between them.

Chapter 33

On Friday night, Mia raised her chin to the ominous SkyView Apartment building, white lights illuminating the top floor, and shuddered. The gleaming high-rise never ceased to be unnerving, especially with her holding a pan of hot lasagna and a dinner reservation with Mr. *Stuffy* Fitzgerald. Although she didn't want to admit it to Bryce, she was ridiculously intimidated by his dad. Of course, this whole dinner thing had been her idea from the start, but she somehow didn't think it through. What on earth would they talk about across the table? Despite her Googling some recent "trends in architecture," Mia knew she was way out of her league on that topic of conversation. Unlike his son, she was positive he wouldn't be even vaguely interested in the fine art of cannoli or biscotti making.

Checking the time, Mia hurried to the revolving door, only to run smack-dab into Eddy, the world's laziest doorman. "Hey. Don't I know you?" he asked, looking her up and down.

"Yes, Eddy. I'm Sal's friend. I saw you just the other day. Remember?" With a huff, she attempted to maneuver around him.

"Oh, yeah. That's right. Bryce's girlfriend." He stretched the arms of his wrinkled jacket above him into a deep yawn, then rubbed his bloodshot eyes.

Mia grumbled, "Whatever," pushing past him into the expansive lobby. When he followed her, she halted and whirled around, opening one of her containers. "Here, Eddy. Want a cannoli cookie or biscotti?" Anything to distract him and leave her alone.

Peeking inside, he frowned. "I wish. Gotta watch my gluten intake."

With a roll of her eyes, Mia asked, "Is Sal around?"

"Nah. He got the night off for his wife's birthday. I'd grab a cookie for him, but he said his doctor wants him to watch his sugar."

Immediately slamming the container shut, Mia tightened her gaze at Eddy. Without another word, she stormed toward the bank of elevators. She pushed the button for the express to the penthouse, like Sal had shown her.

"Say 'hi' to the Fitzgeralds for me," Eddy yelled as the elevator shut.

"This is *not* a good omen," she muttered, closing her eyes and resting against the back of the elevator. If this were any indication of how the rest of the evening would go, she was in trouble. Sucking in a deep breath, she absently adjusted the matching belt of her favorite blue sweater dress.

When the elevator opened to the 30th floor, Mia lunged for the double doors before losing her nerve. Reaching for the doorbell as she balanced her containers, she noticed her bike helmet swinging loosely from her arm. Groaning, she turned back and faced the shiny elevator door. Her well-worn sneakers stared back at her. "Good grief," she moaned at her mismatched reflection. Flopping onto the plush carpeted doormat, she swapped out her sneakers for black leather ankle boots. She pushed herself back up with a *grunt* and crammed the helmet into her overstuffed bag.

Mia gave her new reflection an approving grin, straightening the bottom of her dress and smoothing out her shiny locks. Again, she pivoted toward the bell. But before she could press it, the lock tumbled open. With her arm still raised, she was greeted by Evelyn's welcoming smile. "Hello, Mia. It's lovely to see you, again."

Dropping her arm and redistributing the weight of her containers, Mia gave her a dumbfounded stare. "But how'd you ...? I mean, I didn't even ring the bell."

"Oh. Sorry about that, dear. They finally installed the security camera, right there." She motioned to the tiny black dome mounted onto the ceiling and pointed directly at the door. "It's an extra precaution, when reliable Sal isn't on."

Mia held back a *groan*, adding this recent humiliation to the growing list for the evening. "Awesome," she said sarcastically, shifting the containers from one arm to the other.

"Let me take those for you. And please come in." While Mia crossed the threshold, she added, "It's so nice of you to do this for Bryce and his dad."

"Mia?" Bryce said, joining them in the foyer. "I could've helped you, *again*."

"It's no biggie," she said, readjusting her jacket and backpack. "At least I remembered the bread this time."

"Why don't you take her jacket, Bryce? I'll get these in the kitchen," Evelyn said, moving past them.

As Bryce helped Mia spin out of her windbreaker, he took in her appearance. "Wow. You look ... incredible." Evelyn turned back long enough to throw a smile their way.

Mia tried to hide her glowing cheeks, "Well, I didn't want you to think I only wear jeans and sneakers, especially at dinner with your dad."

His face grew slightly pale. "Actually, Mia. About that—"

"Bryce, who is this?" Mia looked up to Carter Fitzgerald's wide hazel eyes, framed by round, black-rimmed glasses. He approached the foyer with his hands in the pockets of his black slacks, wearing a matching black dress shirt. "Oh. The tutor," he answered himself when he came into the light.

Bryce rested his hand gently on Mia's shoulder. "Dad, you remember my *friend*, Mia?" he asked, with emphasis.

Propelling herself forward, Mia extended her hand without hesitation, like she'd rehearsed. "Lovely to see you again, Mr. Fitzgerald."

Bryce's dad slowly removed his hand from his pocket and accepted hers, raising his eyebrows at her strong handshake. "Welcome. What brings you to our neck of the—"

"Dad, Mia was gracious enough to make dinner for *us*. Lasagna, right?" Bryce asked, turning to her with hopeful eyes.

Confused by her assumed impromptu visit, she said, "Um, yes. My great-great-grandmother's recipe. She was from Sicily. I've been making it for years. Everyone seems to like it." Mentally smacking herself for providing way too much information, she grew silent.

"I'm sure we'll love it." Bryce gave her shoulder a gentle squeeze.

Pausing for a beat to take in the information, his dad simply nodded, waving them farther inside.

Bryce led her through the spacious living room, where Mia turned to him and hissed, "Seriously? He had no idea?"

"Please just go with it, Mia," he whispered, tightening his grip on her shoulder as they met Evelyn in the kitchen.

Twenty minutes later, they surrounded the formal glass dining table, filled with a colorful salad bowl, steaming plates of lasagna, and homemade Italian bread. "You want to join us, Evelyn?" Bryce's dad asked. "This could feed an army."

"Oh, no. Thank you, Carter. I have some laundry to get in. But thank you, Mia. I will be happy to heat some up later."

As Evelyn dashed through the living room and down a hallway, Bryce pulled out a chair for Mia with a wink. They perched atop their firm, upholstered seats in silence that was finally broken by Bryce. "This is delicious, Mia."

"Oh, yes. Definitely," his dad added.

After a few more beats of quiet, Mia said, "Actually. If you think this is a lot of food, you should see our Thanksgivings. Lasagna is only a part of it."

Carter looked up from his plate with a curious expression. "You don't have turkey?"

"Of course. But that comes after the antipasto, soup, lasagna, and ..." She trailed off, seeing a dazed look of bewilderment on Carter's face.

"Sounds like an epic meal," Bryce said.

"Followed by an even more epic and necessary nap," his dad added coolly.

When the uncomfortable silence resumed, Mia did some mental knuckle cracking. Abruptly dropping her fork, she turned to Mr. Fitzgerald. "So, Bryce says you're an architect. That's neat. What do you design?"

Looking up from his lasagna, he adjusted his glasses. "Commercial mostly."

When Mia gave him a blank stare, Bryce clarified, between bites, "No residential. He does a lot of office buildings and luxury retail. His real interest is academic, though. Right, Dad?"

Centering his water glass on his coaster, he answered, "Um, yes. I enjoy designing libraries and academic institutions."

Mia nodded and nibbled on a cheesy noodle, now reminded this conversation was way over her head. Bryce slid a glance at her studying her plate and broke the silence yet again. "His next project is the new science and technology center in the heart of downtown."

Perking up, Mia's blue eyes sparkled. "The one with the astronomy center and research labs?"

"Hopefully," Carter started. "*If* we can get the budget approved."

Bryce turned to his dad. "Mia is quite the science and math whiz. She'd probably love a tour at some point."

Finishing his lasagna, his dad pushed his plate to the side. "Of course. That's right. I must say, you've done a wonderful job getting Bryce up to speed with his classes. All his teachers and coaches are quite impressed. Hopefully, all A's once again, right?" he asked his son, patting him on the back.

"Sure, Dad. Mia's a fantastic teacher."

Her face warming to a bright shade of scarlet, Mia smiled, enjoying another forkful of lasagna.

"Well, everyone at Wellington seems impressed, too. It was only a small indiscretion, after all. Nothing that can't be forgiven, or so the trustees just said."

Mia looked up from her plate, dropping her fork with a loud *clink*. As her heart started beating out of her chest, she took a hard swallow of lasagna. "Um, what?" she croaked, now staring in shock at Bryce.

Chapter 34

Abruptly standing and collecting his plate, Bryce announced, "How about some dessert? Mia brought some amazing cookies for you to try, Dad." He disappeared into the kitchen without uttering another word.

"Oh, yes. The bakery. How long have you been in business?" Carter asked.

Moving her remaining lasagna aimlessly around her plate with a nub of bread, Mia muttered, "Since 1919."

"That is impressive. It's hard for small businesses to stay afloat for all those years. Your family must be doing something right."

Sighing, she continued to play with her food until Bryce returned with a container and pushed it toward his dad. "Try a cookie. Mia made these herself. She's always thinking up new ideas for the bakery."

He hesitated, then finally decided on a pistachio biscotti, sampling a minuscule bite. "Wow. These are nice." Going for another bite, he paused, hearing the phone chime in his pocket. "Sorry," he said, glancing at the screen. "I need to take this. Excuse me." As Mr. Fitzgerald rushed out of the dining room, Mia stared at the remnants of the discarded cookie on his plate.

With dinner clearly over, she rose from the table, bringing her plate into the kitchen. "I should go," she said, starting for the door.

Bryce caught up with her in the foyer. "Do you have to? I know we have a game in the morning, but we could watch a movie or something for a bit."

Mia faced him, her eyes narrowed and hard. "Why didn't you tell me you were going back to Wellington?"

Bowing his head, he shuffled his feet. "Mia, nothing's been decided yet."

Crossing her arms, she focused her steely eyes on him. "I don't know, Bryce. Might want to tell that to your dad. Seems pretty 'decided' to me." She pivoted on the spot and grabbed her backpack and jacket.

"Mia, please don't leave like this. This was such a nice thing you tried."

"Keyword, Bryce: 'tried.' And, clearly failed. As in, crash and burn, right into Wellington Prep." He reached for her arm, but she swatted him away.

"I swear I didn't know he was gonna bring up Wellington. We haven't talked about it since ..."

He stopped himself as she spun around, her heart pounding. "Since *when*?"

Bryce expelled a long sigh and muttered, "Since my old coach called. He heard how well things were going at GW and wanted to chat."

"Of course, he did." With trembling hands, Mia dug into her backpack for her shoes and helmet. "The thing is, I'm partially responsible for you going back. How's that for irony?"

Facing him, she said softly, "I thought we were . . . Nothing. Never mind. I clearly misjudged everything." *Me and everyone else,* she thought. "I'm such an idiot. You can put that in your journal, although you probably already have."

"Mia, don't say that." Speeding up her exit, she gathered both pairs of shoes and lunged for the door. When she reached for the handle with full hands, her unzipped backpack slipped off her shoulder and fell to the floor. Bending over to help her, Bryce spotted some orange inside. He reached into her bag, pulling out the Nerf football. "You brought it back," he said, cracking a smile.

"I didn't know if you wanted to . . . Never mind. You can keep it."

Grabbing his jacket, he beat her to the door. "Give me fifteen minutes, okay? Please."

Mia grudgingly followed Bryce out of the apartment and down a few blocks. And, for fifteen minutes, they tossed the football back and forth in absolute silence, under the radiance of the park lights and a full autumn moon. Occasionally, she would throw a spiral so spirited it made a loud smacking sound against his palms. Looking at her watch, she waved him in. "There. You got your fifteen minutes, okay?" She scooped her backpack off the plush turf and headed toward the exit as Bryce followed closely behind.

"I guess I'm not the only one who gets out my frustrations on the football." He paused, then said softly, "I did that a lot after my mom passed."

Mia remained quiet, unsure how to respond. Her mind was overwhelmed, the revelations of the evening still swirling around in her head. Was this the last time she'd be tossing around the football with Bryce? A painful, undefined emotion burned deep in her chest, making it hard to breathe.

When they reached Mia's bike, parked in front of SkyView, Bryce said, "Thanks for warming up my arm. You're coming tomorrow, right?"

"Of course. I wouldn't miss supporting the team."

He sighed, tossing the ball above his head. "You mean Zach and Logan. Not me."

"I mean you too, Bryce." *More than you know.* Pulling her bike helmet from her backpack, a bright blue paper flew out and sailed toward Bryce, who swiftly caught it and scanned it from top to bottom.

"What's this? Literary magazine? You wrote something to get published?"

Mia vigorously shook her head as she slipped on her helmet. "Uh, no. If you saw me in English class, you'd know that was the worst idea ever."

"What is this, then?"

"Another one of my dumb ideas. Don't worry about it." She reached for the paper.

But Bryce held on to the flyer. "Mia, tell me."

Adjusting her helmet strap, she hesitated. "I thought it was something you could do ... for your mom."

"What'd you mean?"

"You're a talented writer, Bryce. I was so moved by what you wrote about your mom in your journal; I kinda felt like I was getting to know her." Mia waited, gauging his reaction. When his eyes softened, she continued, "You wanted to know what you could do to keep her memory alive. Honestly, I can't think of anything better than writing about her and sharing it."

He took a moment to digest her comments. "You want me to write something about my mom and have it published, for *everyone* to read?"

"Um, I know your journal is private. Well, it should have been—sorry, again. I thought . . . Never mind. Forget it." Mia lunged for the paper, but Bryce was holding it up to the moonlight, reading the details.

"Wait. It says Monday is the deadline."

"I know, Bryce. It's a stupid idea. Please just forget I butted in, again."

She was about to grab the flyer when she noticed his eyes, serious and unwavering, on the printed words. "Thank you, Mia," he said quietly into the paper.

"Um, you're welcome," she said timidly, still trying to assess his thoughtful expression. Focusing her attention back on her helmet strap, she exclaimed, "Argh! Are football helmets this annoying?"

Bryce laughed and pocketed the flyer. "I actually think they're easier. Here, let me." He reached forward with a gentle hand toward her strap.

As he grazed her cheek, sending a tingle all the way down her spine, Mia backed away. "Uh, that's okay. I got it."

"You sure?"

"Yup," she said, fumbling with the buckle a few more times until it clicked. "All set. And, uh, good luck tomorrow."

"Thanks, Mia." He smiled but still had a pensive, distant look about him as she mounted her bike.

Before pedaling off, she grumbled, "Well, time to go figure out how to make something taste decent without sugar and gluten." Bryce lifted his brows, then grimaced. "Yeah, I know. Maybe *I'm* the one who needs the luck."

Chapter 35

"Excuse me!" Mia shouted, pushing her way through the large crowd corralled in front of the bleachers. Still sporting her bike helmet and lugging a plastic container, she was beyond relieved to see her friend saving her a seat.

"Hey, boss! You finally made it. It's the second quarter already." Harper snickered at her helmet. "You gonna join the guys on the field?"

Mia slipped off her helmet and threw it onto the bleachers beside her. "Real funny. This old thing has been driving me nuts. Anyway, you're lucky my legs didn't fall off, pedaling so fast. And what's up with these playoff games being so far away? It was a nice ride along the lake—don't get me wrong. But I swear it took me an extra twenty minutes."

"Well, you know. Gotta keep these games in 'neutral territory,'" Harper mimicked, in air quotes.

"Neutral territory? Whatever. This is way closer to the Lakeshore Hawks than us." Mia passed Harper the container and wriggled out of her jacket.

"Is this why you're so late?" she asked, holding up the container. "Why'd you get up early to bake knowing we had a stupid morning game?"

"I didn't. Didn't even sleep much anyway. Was up all night, until I fell asleep in front of the oven."

"Mia, I love you. But you need to get out more. Stuck in your kitchen on a Friday night? Really?"

Peering over the crowd, Mia took in the sprawling field for the first time. "I wasn't, though. Was at Bryce's..." she said, trailing off at her unintended revelation.

"Oh, really? Care to share?"

Ignoring Harper's smirk, Mia fixed her gaze on the scoreboard. "0-7? What the heck? How are we already down to the Hawks?"

"Because these guys are just like their mascot suggests. Their eyes haven't left Bryce's arm, and they block every pass he's thrown. But you can tell he's getting ticked off and starting to rush more."

Even from the bleachers, Mia could see the determination in their star quarterback's eyes. He'd managed to move the ball another 15 yards for a first down and was pushing harder with only a couple of minutes to go in the half. "Those guys are huge!" she exclaimed, taking in the hulking defensive line.

"I know! They even dwarf Zach and Bryce. And they're relentless. Our guys need to do a better job of protecting our quarterback, 'cause they're after him big time."

The menacing look in their opponents' eyes made Mia squirm in her seat. She knew Bryce could sense it too, because once he received the snap, he wound up ready to throw, only to give up and rush forward through the large pack. "They *are* blocking all our receivers!"

"Yup. Wow, these are fantastic!" Harper exclaimed, practically inhaling a whole muffin. "What are these two kinds?"

Mia stayed focused on Bryce's silhouette. "Pineapple upside-down cake and blueberry caraway seed. I used agave syrup, instead of sugar."

"You're kidding! Where'd you get the idea for such fancy ingredients?"

She shrugged. "Watching way too much *Great British Baking Show.*"

"Well, I'm not a big sugar-free person, but these are amazing. Chloe's gonna flip. Her grandpa would love them."

Mia tore her eyes from the field and skimmed the crowded stadium. "Where *is* Chloe?"

"With Abbie and the girls." Harper pointed a fresh muffin at the row of cheerleaders in front of the bleachers, waving shiny blue and gold pompoms at the field. "Apparently, she's crushing big time on someone, but there's some kind of obstacle. That's all I heard, but you know Chloe. Always *very* dramatic."

Shifting uncomfortably in her seat, Mia studied the tight cluster of girls, huddled in between cheers. It was easy to spot an animated Chloe, deeply engaged and whispering into Abbie's eager ear. "Um, are you guys good with coming over on Friday for girls' night and baking?"

"Of course. Should be fun to catch up. Someone needs to spill the dirt on the cute quarterback." With a wink, she popped the rest of her muffin into her mouth.

Back on the field, the enormous digital clock illuminated only seconds until halftime. When Bryce caught the next snap, his eyes flicked from receiver to receiver. With his path blocked, he remained stationary, desperately searching for a way forward. Taking advantage of the rare opportunity, the Hawks' defensive line charged for him, ultimately slamming Bryce hard on his back.

The loud *smack* of bodies and helmets reverberated against the stadium's metal bleachers, leaving Mia to recoil in her seat. All around her, the crowd jumped to its feet in a collective gasp as the tackle pile slowly peeled away, revealing Bryce's limp body on the very bottom.

"They did *not* just sack our quarterback!" Harper warned, crossing her arms.

"Is he okay?" Mia said in barely a whisper while crumpled up in a tight ball.

With wobbly legs, she unfurled herself and rose onto her toes, peeking around the chaotic crowd. Cupping her trembling hand to shield against the morning sunshine, Mia squinted into the distance, hoping to catch a glimpse of Bryce's sparkling hazel eyes through his facemask. But he continued to remain frighteningly still on the ground. When the trainers and Coach Warner ran onto the field, it became clear this wasn't just a simple tackle. As Zach frantically raced over to his motionless teammate, Mia started to panic, her heart hammering against her chest. With Bryce surrounded on the field, the cheerleaders' mood turned subdued as they kneeled on the ground for their seemingly injured quarterback.

Chapter 36

For several minutes, an uncomfortable silence enveloped the crowd. Mia could barely hold herself back from the field, watching the dramatic scene unfold in slow motion. "Please get up, Bryce," she pleaded, shutting her eyes.

Harper wrapped an arm around her. "Mia, I'm sure he'll be fine. Coach Warner and the trainers are the best."

"What if he has a concussion? Or worse?" she croaked as the colored warmth leached from her face.

Finally, when Mia couldn't stand the suspense any longer, the circle around Bryce parted as he appeared to sit up. With the help of Coach Warner, Zach, and the roaring crowd, he rose from the field, and she was finally able to breathe. Still appearing stunned, Bryce headed for the bench, where he sat out the last few seconds of the half.

When the clock eventually ran out, Mia jumped up, ready to head to the field. But a crew of trainers whisked Bryce off toward the locker room before she had a chance to blink. "Where are they taking him?" she moaned to Harper.

"Mia, they probably want to check him out some more. That was a hard hit he took. Come on. We'll wait out halftime by the field."

"Hey, guys!" Chloe said, happily greeting them when they'd reached the cheerleaders. Her face fell, noticing her friend's colorless cheeks. "Mia, you okay?"

"She's worried about Bryce," Harper easily volunteered, and Mia cringed.

Chloe gave her a comforting pat on the back. "Zach went with him, so we'll know something soon."

Mia spent most of halftime chewing on her fingernails and pacing in front of the bleachers. When Zach finally appeared from the locker room, she was practically on his heels, charging up to the sidelines. "Hey, Mia. Good to see you," he cheerfully greeted her.

She gave him a quick hug, followed by a concerned, "Is he okay?"

"Bryce? Yeah. They checked him out. No concussion. Just got the wind knocked out of him. Poor guy couldn't breathe for a while there."

"He wasn't the only one," she said, feeling her chest relax.

Zach gently squeezed her shoulder. "He's gonna be fine. Probably a few bruises from those jerks. And Coach definitely gave us a nice refresher on the importance of 'protecting the quarterback.' But he'll be out soon for the second half."

"What? He's still gonna play?"

As the words flew out of her mouth, Bryce emerged from the locker room. He was grinning and chatting beside an elated Coach Warner, like nothing out of the ordinary had happened. When the crowd spotted him, applause and cheers erupted around Mia as she stared in disbelief. Bryce appeared to be his normal self, albeit with several bloody scrapes on his arms he seemed content to ignore.

"See, Mia? He's fine," Zach said, heading for the huddle. She crossed her arms and returned to the stands in a huff.

While still ticked off at the start of the second half, Mia had to admit Coach Warner's locker room speech must have been an inspirational display. When GW's defensive line faced Lakeshore's quarterback for the first play of the third quarter, to say they were beating them at their own game was an understatement. No matter what Lakeshore did, GW blocked it.

As soon as Bryce returned to the field, Mia kept a keen eye on him. When he received the first snap, she noticed his normal take charge attitude replaced by hesitation. Looking carefully at his eyes, darting between the charging defensive line and any available receiver, she wondered if she'd seen some fear in them. *Just rush, Bryce. Go for it,* she thought. Instead, he threw a tight and risky pass to Zach. Unfortunately, one of Lakeshore's giant linemen leapt in front of him and caught the ball for an easy interception. Although the Eagles stopped him after only a few yards, the damage was already done. Mia could see it on Bryce's face as he ripped off his helmet, stomping to the sidelines. Zach gave him a pat on the back, but it was clear Bryce was livid.

"What is going on with him?" Harper moaned.

Mia pondered that herself, studying Zach and Bryce having an intense conversation on the bench. "Hopefully, Zach can snap him out of it."

"These are fantastic, Mia," Chloe said, munching on a blueberry muffin. With all the drama happening on the field, she had eagerly joined them in the stands after the first half. "Mind if I take some for my grandpa?"

"Oh, sure," Mia said, coming out of her trance. "By the way, tell your mom I'm still working on the gluten-free thing. Let's just say the dough's not so easy to work with."

Suddenly, the crowd around them sprang up as the Eagles intercepted the Hawks' ball. When Bryce enthusiastically bounded from the bench toward the line of scrimmage, he looked like a different quarterback. This time, when he received the snap, his eyes quickly glazed over his blocked receivers. Without missing a beat, he charged through the defensive line for a 40-yard rush. Zach slapped him a high-five as they lined up for the next play. Again, with most receivers blocked, Bryce looked to his favorite running back for the fake, then raced around a confused defense all the way to the end zone.

Moments later, Harper screamed, "Go, Logan!" when he finished a perfect kick through the uprights, to tie up the low-scoring game by the end of the third quarter.

The game continued to be low scoring, the offense taking a backseat to the two teams' impressive defensive lines. When Bryce returned to the field for the game's final minutes, he appeared exasperated. Now, absolutely covered in mud from the morning dew with scrapes on all his limbs, he looked like he'd been through a battle. Not to mention, all his running attempts were exhausting.

So much so, it didn't surprise Mia when he gunned the ball directly to Zach on the next play, in lieu of another grueling rush. When Zach caught it a few yards short of the end zone, Bryce looked not only relieved but thrilled. Unfortunately, even that close to the goal line, the defense was pulling out all stops. With only one down to go, Coach Warner decided to lean on his reliable kicker, with a less risky field goal attempt.

"Come on, Logan. You can do this," Harper muttered under her breath, gripping Mia's arm so tightly it was bound to leave a bruise.

Logan loosened himself up, hopping up and down and practicing a few air kicks. Taking a steadying breath, he backed up and kicked the ball squarely through the uprights. As his teammates tackled his tiny silhouette to the ground in celebration, Harper giggled and shot him an enthusiastic thumbs-up.

"Maybe *someone* should spill on the adorable kicker and all those one-on-one practice sessions," Mia teased, elbowing a red-faced Harper.

Thankfully, the clock ran out as the Hawks started another aggressive move down the field. In one large wave, the Eagles fans poured out of the stands toward their team, now bumping chests and slapping high-fives. Mia found Zach first, wrapping her arms around him. "OMG, Zach! That way too close! But major congrats!"

"I know, right? Only a three-point win, but who cares? We're going to the finals!" he cheered, jumping up and down like a kid on Christmas morning.

In the heart of the chaos, Bryce was fully surrounded and receiving accolades from most of the student section and cheer squad. As his eyes swept the stadium and eventually rested on Mia, he offered a coy smile and a little wave. He pushed past the remaining crowd, surprising her with a tight embrace of football pads and filthy jersey. "Hey. You made it," he whispered into her ear.

Mia immediately absorbed his comforting warmth, moving from the tips of her ponytail down to her toes. "Are you okay?"

Slowly pulling away, he slipped off his scuffed helmet. "Yeah. I won't lie; I'm pretty beat up. But they say I'll live. Thanks to this thing." Beaming, he affectionately smacked his helmet. "See? Not just annoying." As Mia took in Bryce's battered helmet and grass-stained uniform, her soft eyes hardened. She shot him a scowl and a swift punch in the arm. "Ouch! What was that for?" he said, rubbing his arm.

"You freaked me out, you jerk! I thought you died out there!"

"Well, if it makes you feel any better, I *felt* like I died. Nothing like a couple minutes of barely breathing to give you some perspective."

Patting his arm lightly, Mia softened her tone. "Sorry. I'm probably grumpy from lack of sleep. Was baking all night, and I'm exhausted."

He gave her a sympathetic look, combing his hand through his damp waves. "You think you still have some energy left to come celebrate? A bunch of us are going out for pizza."

"I'd like to, Bryce. But I should get back to the grind. Some really awful gluten-free recipes are waiting for me to mess them up."

He nodded as disappointment flitted across his face. "Oh. Well, good luck. And thanks for coming."

"Sure. And thanks for sharing." She chuckled, brushing off dried mud and grass he'd deposited onto her sweater.

"Anytime." Scanning the crowd, he asked, "By the way, have you seen Chloe?"

Mia looked up from her sweater with surprise in her eyes. "Um, yeah. She was sitting with us. I think I saw her talking with Abbie as we left the bleachers."

"Oh, great. I'll go find her. See you later, okay?" he said with a smile, gently tugging her long ponytail.

She tried to smile back. But, watching Bryce take off toward Chloe, an uncomfortable feeling started forming deep in the pit of her stomach.

Chapter 37

"So, Harper. Time to give us the dirt on you and Logan," Mia said, taking the popcorn out of the microwave.

"Um. Maybe we should wait until Chloe gets back." She focused her attention on pouring three glasses of soda. "I'm starving after all this baking. I don't know how you do it."

Mia sighed at the kitchen counters, cluttered with long rows of biscotti and shortbread cookies. "I know. The thing is, there's so much more to do. I'm still laminating that dough in the fridge, and we haven't even started on the cannoli cookies. Argh!" she exclaimed, covering her face with her hands. "Whose crazy idea was this anyway?"

"Ah, that would be yours, boss. Remember?" Harper gave her arm a gentle pat. "Listen. We'll take a short dinner break and then get back at it. We have all day tomorrow too, before the sale on Sunday."

Mia sucked in a calming breath. "Gotcha. Good plan."

Chloe bounded through the door with a large pizza box, cutting into Mia's almost Zen moment. "You two should've seen the delivery guy downstairs! *So cute!*" she gushed, carefully squeezing the box on the already-crowded countertop. "Mia, your parents said to take our time, 'destroying the kitchen,' I think they said. So, anyway, they're going out for a late dinner."

Harper dived into the pizza box. "You think we can fit in a nap before we continue this baking marathon? I'm exhausted from passing out flyers around town all day."

"Sure, she'll give us a little break. Right, Mia?" Chloe batted her eyelashes and elbowed a stoic Mia, who answered with an eye roll.

Scooping up the popcorn bowl, Mia moved the girls' night into the living room, where they collapsed onto the pile of fluffy sleeping bags. "Anyway, it's time for Harper to share about her favorite kicker." She dug into the popcorn as Chloe's eyes magnified through her glasses.

Harper provided her own effective eye roll, snagging another slice of pizza. "Good grief, guys. We're just *friends*."

"Oh! Poor Logan! He's been permanently *friend-zoned*!" Chloe giggled so hard she almost dropped her slice of pepperoni.

Mia joined Chloe in her contagious laughter. "Whatevs, Harper. We saw how happy you were with his, um, kicking?"

"You guys are impossible!" she exclaimed, falling back onto her sleeping bag. "Seriously, Logan's awesome, but it's probably best if he stays in the *zone*. But maybe it's time Chloe spilled about her new crush!"

Ignoring her, Chloe clicked on the TV. "Mia, do you have the History Channel? There's supposed to be this great documentary on the pyramids."

"Um. No, idea. Maybe check the guide," she said, laughing to herself.

As Chloe flipped through the channels, Harper turned to Mia. "Speaking of friends, what about you and our hot quarterback?"

Mia almost choked on her soda. But, before she could answer, Chloe's phone buzzed, sending her rifling through her pockets. Smiling at the screen, she declared, "Gotta get this. Be right back," running off to Mia's bedroom and slamming the door.

"What was that all about?" Mia asked. Harper yawned and shimmied into her sleeping bag. "Probably the new crush. I think they met up after the game last weekend."

"Oh?" As Mia stared down at her pizza, an uneasy feeling whirling through her gut. "Did she tell you anything else about him?"

Harper pulled her sleeping bag up to her chin with another yawn. "Nope. Just that he's *dreamy*, apparently. Oh, and she's worried about people finding out." Closing her eyes, she muttered, "Only a few minutes, okay. Then, I promise I'll bake until dawn." Within seconds, she was sound asleep, and Mia collected the plates and pizza box.

Mia was loading the dishwasher when Chloe returned with bright cheeks and a grin she couldn't seem to contain. Seeing Harper snoring away in the living room, she let out a surprised giggle. "What the heck did I miss? She's comatose."

Smiling, Mia searched through a drawer for the aluminum foil. "I think she clocked several miles today, passing out those bake sale flyers. She's doing a great job as committee chair."

"True. Oh, let me help." Chloe grabbed the foil and started wrapping up the leftover pizza. "So, um, haven't talked much lately. Well, with Bryce taking up all your time in science class. What's up with you guys, really?" she asked casually.

Mia closed the dishwasher, relaxing against it. "Honestly, it's complicated." *Really complicated,* she thought, cutting her eyes at Chloe.

"But it does look like you guys have a lot of fun together. Mia, you sure it's not *more* than you think?"

Giving her friend a serious look, she asked frankly, "Would you be mad if it was?"

Chloe looked up from the pizza box with eyes as wide as her frames. "Of course not. I'd be thrilled."

Mia was taken aback. "Wait. I thought ... I thought *you* liked him."

Chloe almost dropped the pizza on the floor on her way to the fridge. "What? No way, Mia. I mean, I think he's cute. But who doesn't? Honestly, he's only had eyes for you since day one."

"Why do people keep saying that?" she moaned, crossing her arms.

"Duh. Because it's true. And I'll have you know he specifically asked me if you and Zach were ever a 'thing.'"

Uncrossing her arms, Mia's mouth fell open. "He did what? When? Why on earth would he ask that?"

"After the game. Because you and Zach are best friends. Come on, Mia. You remember when people used to tease you two in elementary school. You were practically inseparable. And there's something else."

"What?"

"Well, I kinda got the feeling he was willing to, you know, *step aside* if he needed to."

"For Zach and me? OMG, that is so awkward!" Mia groaned with her head in her hand. "He's like my older brother. Sure, he's adorable. But, I mean, it's Zach."

Chloe giggled, pouring herself a refill. "I'll remember to tell *him* that. Seriously, though. Do *you* like Bryce?"

"I don't know. It's all so confusing. It's like, we have a great time hanging out, but his life is so different from mine. He actually has a housekeeper who does his laundry. And don't get me started on his stuffy dad." Then, she lowered her eyes to the floor. "Plus, he might be going back to Wellington."

"Mia, I'm sure you know him better. But none of that stuff seems important to him. And it does look like he's interested in getting to know you."

"Chloe, it's not quite what you think."

"What do you mean?"

"Let's just say I've gotten some insight into what he really thinks."

Chloe paused, letting her comments sink in. "Is that where some of the 'complicated' and 'confusing' comes in?"

Desperately needing a change in subject, Mia said, "Well, enough with my interrogation. What's up with this crush? Do we get to meet him?"

With her glass mid-sip Chloe froze, then gulped it down with a shrug. "Um, maybe." When Harper's snoring reached jackhammer level, Chloe blew out a sigh and strolled into the living room. "In the meantime, I think all of us deserve a couple hours of shut-eye before the all-night baking begins. What do you say?"

Mia nodded and yawned. "I'll set the alarm."

Chapter 38

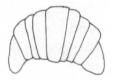

"Oh, no! No, no, no, no. It can't be!" Mia exclaimed, staring at the glowing clock numbers on her cell phone. "Guys, get up!"

Slowly sitting up in her sleeping bag, Harper yawned and stretched out her arms. "What time is it?"

"It's almost noon!" Mia shouted, jumping out of her constricting covers.

Harper's eyes sprang open in disbelief. "No way, Mia. We couldn't have slept that long."

"Well, this says we did!" She shoved her phone screen at Harper, who leapt up, running into the bathroom without another word. Kicking Chloe's shin, Mia yelled, "Time to get up. We have to finish the baking!"

Chloe shrank even deeper into her bag. "We have plenty of time, Mia. Your alarm hasn't gone off. And it's so warm and cozy in here."

"Argh, Chloe!" Mia howled, tugging at her sleeping bag. "We overslept. I must have messed up the alarm or slept through it."

Slowly emerging from the depths of her bag, Chloe reached for her glasses on the coffee table with a *snort*. "We have all day, Mia. How much more baking could there possibly be?"

Rushing into her bedroom to change, she yelled back, "Believe me, Chloe. Plenty. If only we had more hands." Suddenly, her face lit up. She pulled out her unreliable phone and texted an SOS message to a *very* reliable Zach.

An hour later, the girls were standing behind the stainless counter in the bakery kitchen, with Mia intricately explaining the fine art of rolling a cornetto. "It's nice of your dad to let us use the kitchen for a few hours, Mia," Chloe said, scowling at her failed attempt at rolling the "little horn" into a croissant shape. "Remind me not to try origami, by the way."

Mia bent over the counter, rerolling her dough. "You're getting there, Chloe. And you guys know how much my dad loves the food bank. Only a simple mention about fundraising for it, and he's totally on board."

Harper raised her arms in victory, crying out, "Yes! Cornetto success!" proudly showing off her rolled results.

"Keep it down, guys," Mia hissed, shushing them. "My dad knows we're baking, but not *what* we're making." She brushed egg wash and sprinkled sugar on another proofed pan and walked it to the oven.

Chloe let out a sigh. "Mia, why not mention some of your recipes and ideas? Your dad is awesome. And, honestly, he thinks you're amazing in everything you do."

Shaking her head, Mia kept her eyes on the oven. "You know why. The bakery is the one place he doesn't like changes or suggestions. This time, everything has to be perfect."

Just then, the door abruptly swung open, revealing Zach's huge grin. "Help has arrived!" he announced.

Mia bolted from the oven, engulfing him in a grateful hug. "Thank you for coming so quickly. We could really use another set of hands."

"What about more than one?" he asked with a wink, holding open the door.

Bryce waltzed in and said, "Or even a few more?" ushering in Logan and several other members of the football team.

Logan instantly moved to Harper's side, looking impressed and giving her next sheet of cornetti a thumbs-up. "Clearly, some of us have no idea what we're doing here. But we'd love to help."

Mia flashed Zach a smile, mouthing, "Thank you."

"Don't look at me," he whispered. "I mentioned to Bryce that I was coming by to help you, and he offered to contact everyone."

A little while later, Mia had her volunteers set up at various stations along the counter, working on different recipes. Bryce was turning into a fantastic source of information, having paid expert attention to her previous lessons. Not only did he know how to roll a cornetto, but he was also a biscotti-making machine and had even perfected exactly how much to fill a cannoli cookie.

As Mia made her way around the counter, keeping a keen eye on the ovens, she stopped by Bryce to compliment his next perfectly rolled and perfectly proofed pan of cornetti. "Thanks for bringing reinforcements," she said softly, helping him brush egg wash on the dough.

He shrugged, sprinkling sugar on top. "No big deal. You support the team all the time. About time we give back." She grabbed the pan and popped it into the oven while Bryce followed. "So, how's the gluten-free thing going?"

"Um, okay," she said, her attention still focused on the oven door. "I have a brownie that might work. Not sure if I'm brave enough to share it yet, especially tomorrow, on such an important occasion."

"Well, I'm sure you'll figure it out." When Mia faced him, their eyes held for a long moment. Bryce closed the space between them and raised his hand to gently brush her cheek. "Flour," he said softly.

"Oh. Thanks," she whispered, feeling the warmth of his hand linger. She scrubbed her cheek with the hem of her apron. "I'm such a mess."

He gave her a sincere smile. "No. Just Mia."

Bryce was about to say something else, when the *beep* of the oven timer filled the room, making Mia jump. Grateful for the reprieve, she turned and pulled the next pan out of the oven. Tossing it onto the counter in one swift move, she bolted past Zach, mumbling, "I need some fresh air."

Breezing past the near-empty bakery, Mia was once again slapped in the face with the reality of the situation and the importance of the next day. Waving to her dad, happily chatting with Mrs. Rossi, she dashed out the door with the *jingle* of a bell.

Stepping out into the brisk air of late autumn, Mia rubbed her arms and slumped to the sidewalk at the foot of the bakery. As she leaned against the cold brick of the building and shut her eyes, she was barely aware of another *jingle* carrying across the block. "Hey. Is this seat available?" Zach asked softly, snapping Mia out of her thoughts.

Opening her eyes, she lifted her chin and nodded. "Of course."

He slipped down beside her, hugging his arms across his chest. "A little chilly out here tonight."

"Yeah. It was getting a bit stifling in there."

"I'm sure everyone is gonna miss you inside. Don't you want to come back?"

Mia shook her head, staring down at the sidewalk. "I'm not sure I can, Zach. Everything's been so overwhelming lately." She aimlessly brushed her cheek. "And confusing."

Zach lightly bopped his knee on hers. "That doesn't sound like my friend, Mia DeSalvo. In fact, my friend Mia is the strongest and bravest person I know."

Drawing her knees up to her chest, she played with the laces of her sneakers. "I doubt that. My life is easy compared to some."

"You really think that? The person who is single-handedly trying to save her parents' business while organizing an amazing fundraiser? Plus, you're a fantastic friend. And don't even get me started on your impressive grades, Mia. None of that is easy."

"It is when you don't lose anyone in the process."

Zach hooked his arm around her. "Do you remember when you tried to teach my dad how to make his favorite almond biscotti in that very same kitchen?"

Mia nodded, cracking a smile. "He made more of a flour mess than I ever could."

"Yeah. And your dad permanently banned him from your kitchen."

"With a big, goofy grin on his face. He was in hysterics at your dad's 'sheer ineptitude in the kitchen,' I think were his words!" They shared a laugh as the wind picked up, flapping the blue canvas awning above and sweeping crunchy leaves past their feet. "It was so much fun though, despite the mess."

As the tone turned more somber, he said, "Mia, you lost someone, too." Zach's words hung heavy in the chilly autumn air, cutting deeply through her—making her shiver.

With a simple shrug, she moved her attention back to her shoelaces.

"Yet, never once did you let me see you sad, Mia. You just kept making food for us and watching Eli—whatever you could do to help. And, when the food bank helped us out, you were there to donate every last loaf of bread to make up the difference."

She looked up with glossy eyes. "You guys made the sacrifices, not me."

"You know that's not true, Mia, especially over the last two years. You always put everyone else first, regardless of what's going on with you. Your parents see it. All your friends see it. And, as much as you're trying to hide it, Bryce sees it, too."

"Zach, don't."

"Why? It's true. You'd tear yourself to pieces to help your friends. Geez, it took only minutes to get everyone together to help you tonight. Why don't you want Bryce to see the *real* you?"

Shaking off his arm, she stood, facing away from him. "Zach, of all people, I thought you had my back with this one. All this stupid talk of me and Bryce."

"I'm just saying you made a difference in Bryce, and you should know that—because *he* knows that." He rose from the sidewalk, brushing off his jeans.

"I tutored him a little. It's no big deal."

"Let me tell you something, Mia. When Bryce showed up that first morning practice, he was an angry, sad guy who didn't care about anything. It was obvious he was glad to get out of boarding school, but every pass of that football carried his anger with it. And then, things started to change. Coach noticed it, and so did I. It was like he was holding this huge weight he suddenly just let go. That's because of you."

"How do you know it was me?" Crossing her arms defiantly, she whipped around and said firmly, "And you'd better not say it."

"Say what?"

"Argh, Zach!" Mia stomped her feet in frustration. "The ridiculous, 'the way he looks at you' thing."

Zach contemplated her comment for a few beats. "I don't know about all that. I mean your friendship. He seems to trust you more than anyone else. Like you know something about him no one else ever could."

"I guess so," she muttered with a shrug. "But it's not as simple as you think, Zach."

"Maybe. And maybe you're making it more complicated than it needs to be."

Mia threw up her hands, giving him an exasperated look. "You realize you speak in riddles half the time when you give advice." Glancing back at the bakery, she said, "So, Mr. Brilliant Advice. What do I do now?"

"Well, you can start by going back in there and facing stuff. Because, honestly, we may win football games, but most of us are absolutely hopeless when it comes to rolling that cornetto thing!"

"Fine. You win." Mia tried not to laugh as she moved toward the door.

As Zach reached for the handle, he looked deep in thought. "Actually. That's interesting." When she wrinkled her forehead, he said, "With you and Bryce. I'm not so sure he's the only one looking."

Chapter 39

Early the next morning, Mia yawned as she smoothed out the "Fundraising Bake Sale" flyers taped to the bakery facade. With only a few hours of sleep, she'd helped her dad load the seemingly never-ending plastic tubs into their bakery van while her mom made sure everyone was comfortable and fully caffeinated inside. Gazing through the glow of the windows that revealed only the handful of customers on a Sunday morning, Mia knew this was her one remaining chance to make a difference.

"Morning, Mia," she heard from a familiar voice, pulling her from her thoughts.

She looked up the deserted street to see Bryce approaching as the sun tickled the horizon. He was bundled up in his hunter-green puffer jacket and matching gloves, his hazel eyes reflecting their color in the early morning light. "Morning," she said with another yawn, tightening her scarf.

"Chilly weather for the bake sale, huh?" He lightly tapped her rosy nose and cheek with his toasty glove. "How long have you been out here?"

"A while, I guess. Helped my dad load the van. He's on his way to the school now, so we should probably get going." She hugged her chest to keep warm, then started in the direction of the school.

Bryce nodded, following her. "Why didn't you ask me to help? You must be exhausted after last night."

She shrugged. "You guys helped enough. And, honestly, if this doesn't go well, I'm sure I'll have many more sleepless nights. Better than my parents, I guess."

He stopped abruptly, turning on his heel to face her. "Mia, why do you always do that?"

"Do what?" She blew on her bare hands, now a deep shade of pink from the morning chill.

"Never think of yourself. I want to help. I'm sure your parents do, too. You're not an island, Mia."

Rolling her eyes and blowing on her hands, yet again, she said, "Geez. If I didn't know any better, I'd say you've been spending way too much time with Zach. That's something he would say." She resumed her brisk walk, and Bryce hurried to catch up.

"Well, he's right. And why don't you have gloves on?"

Stopping again, she moaned, "I thought this was supposed to be a nice, relaxing walk, Bryce. I didn't realize you wanted an early-morning interrogation. And, if you must know, I couldn't find them, okay? I'm a *mess*, remember?" She took off again, leaving him behind.

"Mia, please stop saying that," he said, catching up to her. When she blew on her hands once more, he groaned and placed them snuggly between his gloves.

"Thanks," she said quietly as the instant warmth moved up to her fingertips. Bryce gently blew warm air between their palms, and she felt her heart flutter.

"See? Not so bad letting someone help, right?"

She slowly nodded, staring down at their hands. Suddenly, the rattle of a gate cut across the quiet block, alerting them that an elderly shopkeeper was opening his store. When he turned toward them and waved, Mia pulled her hands free. Bryce let out a long sigh as she pocketed them into her jacket. "Hey, Mr. Phillips. Nice morning," she said to the shopkeeper, speeding up their walk.

"It is, indeed, Mia. Have a lovely day," he said, disappearing inside.

Passing another tranquil block, their arms brushed against each other. "So, how do you feel about today?" Bryce asked.

Mia exhaled a chilly puff of air, watching the sun's orange beams lift past the horizon. "I don't know. A bit nervous, I guess."

"About your dad or the bake sale?"

She mulled over his question. "It's hard to put into words."

"What do you mean?" he asked, studying her with interest.

"Well, when you create something and share it with others, there's always a chance people won't like it. It's hard not to take it personally when you put so much of yourself into it."

"I get that," he said without hesitation. Mia raised her chin, looking into his eyes with curiosity. "But sometimes it's worth the risk, right?"

"I hope so, Bryce," she said, heaving a heavy sigh. "Because if this doesn't work, I've completely run out of ideas." Focusing out into the distance, she was lost in her own thoughts for the rest of their walk.

When they reached the edge of the football stadium, brimming with students and volunteers, Mia was floored by the turnout. *They all came. This might actually work,* she thought, a smile thawing her frozen cheeks.

As they headed for the 50-yard line, where a gigantic gold eagle was meticulously painted on the freshly mowed grass, Mia spotted Harper, clipboard in hand. "Hey, guys! Good morning," she said, tucking some unruly wisps of hair inside her knitted beanie.

"Wow! Everything looks fantastic," Mia said as they toured the long line of tables skimming the field.

Harper held up several sheets of paper with color-coded notes. "Well, it's all your plan, boss. We're simply following it. Oh, and your dad unloaded your stuff on your table with all the baked goods. He said he'll be back later."

"Thanks, Harper," Mia said, locating a table in the distance, marked "DeSalvo Bakery."

"Yup. No prob. And we have someone donating heaters until the sun warms things up—another one of your great ideas, Mia." Angling close, she whispered, "FYI, Urban Coffee was the first to show. They're almost all set up if you want to, I don't know, check it out." Harper gave her a wink as she walked away.

Arriving at Mia's assigned table, she quickly found her backpack tucked under it. She unzipped her bag and pulled out a new blue binder filled with bright color-coded tabs.

"Hmm. This looks vaguely familiar," Bryce teased, holding up the binder.

She snatched it from his hands. "Maybe, a little." Dropping it onto the table, she flipped to the section labeled "Bake Sale."

"What is all this?" He thumbed through the various tabs, marked with everything from "Recipes" to "Financials," and even "Marketing."

"Just put some of my ideas in a more formal version, for my dad."

"Mia, this looks like a business plan. My dad had one of these done for his firm. How did you figure all this out?"

"I don't know. Googled 'Business Plan?'" she answered with a shrug and a wink.

Turning her attention from her binder, she draped a dark blue tablecloth, the exact shade of the bakery logo, over the barren brown table. Then, she started opening containers and placing items into groups behind carefully crafted identification cards, printed in the same bakery blue. Bryce followed her every move as she pulled out a stack of what appeared to be business cards with the bakery logo. He held one up to the sunlight, looking intrigued. "They're easy to make," she said. "You can get a ton online really cheap."

He shot her a sarcastic look. "Yeah. I'm sure all of this is *easy*." Admiring her impressive display of containers, he found one still closed on the ground, near the table. "Oh. You forgot this one."

Before Mia could grab it, he opened it to find it stuffed full of fudgy brownies. "These smell amazing. Wait. Are these the gluten-free ones?"

Taking the container from him, she immediately closed it with a definitive *snap*. "Yeah. My dad must have accidentally grabbed it with the other containers."

"Can I try one?"

She hesitated, then reluctantly reopened the plastic tub. "Fine."

As he took a large bite of moist, rich brownie, she instinctively held her breath. "These really are gluten-free? They're the best brownies I've ever had."

Mia couldn't help but smile. But she shook it off, snapping the top closed, once again. "Aren't you the one who said he isn't the expert?"

Bryce's eyes swept the table filled with a large variety of baked goods, from sugar-packed to sugar-free. "What exactly does your dad think you're here selling today?"

"The usual bakery stuff. He even gave me some of his cannoli, which I'm happy to report tastes just like our cookies."

"But he doesn't have a clue these are *your* recipes?"

Her smile fading, she said firmly, "No. I told you. I'm not ready yet."

"Mia, you have nothing to worry about. He's gonna love all this stuff because it came from you. Who wouldn't?"

Even with the chilly morning, Mia felt unexpected heat creep up her cheeks. Lifting the brownie container, she viewed it with different eyes. "I guess I could leave these out for a little while. See if anyone is interested. Since I put so much time into them."

Bryce beamed and opened the container, popping another morsel of brownie into his mouth. "I couldn't agree more."

Chapter 40

Within a couple of hours, the food bank bake sale was bustling. Between the flyers Harper had handed out across town and word of mouth from students and volunteers, everyone seemed eager to satisfy their sweet tooth by 10 a.m. Mia was excited to see so many of her classmates stopping by her table and supporting the great cause. They seemed especially thrilled to catch a glimpse of their new star quarterback's prized dimples.

With Bryce busy selling cookies to his endearing fans, Mia ventured out to the rest of the tables. Earlier, she'd casually strolled by Urban Coffee's loud, green masterpiece. The table was overflowing with gigantic chocolate croissants and tiny, overpriced cookies. Behind it stood life-size posters of overly cheerful people, enjoying frothy beverages and, *apparently*, nonstop jokes.

When Mia passed by the table yet again, she sneered at the enormous beaming faces glaring back at her. "Good morning! Would you like to try a sample?" she heard from behind the table. When a red head emerged from below with a new sleeve of tiny green cups, he gave her a questioning look. "Hey. You're Chloe's friend, right?"

Doing a double take, Mia crossed her arms. "Yeah. How do you know Chloe?"

Looking uncomfortable for a moment, he answered innocently, "Um, you know. She likes chai lattes."

Mia was still giving him a side-eye when she heard a voice behind her. "Hey, guys. What's up? Mia, you remember Seth, right?" Chloe asked, smiling a little too wide.

Her blue eyes piercing through Seth's pristine green apron, Mia grumbled, "Sure. How could I forget?"

With the awkward silence filling the air, Seth shoved a tray between them. "Uh, chai latte sample?"

"No, thank you," Mia said, between clenched teeth. Chloe downed a quick cup, waved, and pulled her away from the table. "Chloe! What the heck was that all about? How much time are you spending at Urban Coffee?"

Chloe focused her gaze uncomfortably on the ground and fiddled with her glasses. "Not *too* much. Seth makes the best chai lattes."

As Mia cut her eyes from Chloe to Seth, who was still staring from his table, her mouth dropped open. *Chloe's hidden crush?* "Oh, no, you didn't, Chloe. Seth? Are you kidding me? Consorting with the enemy?"

"But he's a nice guy and doesn't even like working at Urban Coffee. His parents own it, so he just helps out like you do at the bakery."

Mia shot Seth a critical look, his smile dissolving as he handed out sample after sample with a pained look in his eyes. "Where does he go to school?"

"Lakeshore. But his parents are sick of that long commute. He's trying to convince them to move. So, if we're lucky, he'll be with us at GW next year."

Mia scoffed at Chloe's comment. "Lucky, huh?"

"Please don't be mad. I promise I haven't said anything about the bakery. Although, he's said plenty about Urban Coffee."

Mia's attention was instantly piqued, her eyebrows shooting sky-high. "Oh, really?"

"Yeah. Like, they don't even make most of their stuff. It's all bought frozen and heated up in the microwave. Although, the lattes are still good."

Mia observed the passers-by, grabbing free latte samples, then swiftly moving on to the next table. "Well, the good news is they aren't selling much. I mean, not for the fundraiser. But most people are only taking those tiny cups and walking away."

"Can't we forget this and enjoy the day? Please, Mia?" Chloe begged.

Still preoccupied with the giant green eyesore of a table in front of her, she said, "Um, what?" eventually snapping herself out of her trance. "Okay. Fine."

"Good. Because I have something special to show you," Chloe said in a singsong voice. Swinging her backpack around, she set it on the ground and pulled out a navy-blue hardcover book. On the front, it said, "George Washington High School, Literary Magazine, Fall Edition," in sparkling gold letters. "Check it out! This is hot off the presses from this morning. It's just the mockup but looks amazing already."

She handed the book to Mia, who ran her fingers over the smooth cover and quickly thumbed through dozens of glossy pages of text. "Chloe, this is awesome and super professional. Congrats!"

"Thanks! We had so many great submissions this year, we're hoping to sell out." Then, looking giddy with excitement, she added, "Especially one *particular* submission." Chloe paused for dramatic effect. Rubbing her hands together, she squealed and pointed to the book. "Mia, check out the first piece, after the 'Table of Contents.'"

Raising her eyebrows at Chloe, Mia opened the book, then flipped past the front matter and gasped. Staring back at her, in heavy black lettering and 12-point font, was the name *Bryce Fitzgerald*. "Wait. He wrote something?" she whispered into the air. She lowered her gaze until her breath caught again—this time at the title: "The Orange Football."

Chapter 41

B ut how?" Mia asked, still unable to believe her eyes. "Bryce came up to me after the Lakeshore game. Said you told him about the submissions. He emailed me later that night with this piece. Honestly, all of us on the editorial board were so floored, we had to put it first. Seriously, didn't even need editing."

Mia's eyes never left the printed page as she muttered, "He's a talented writer."

"That's for sure." Then, Chloe lowered her voice. "Just keep it confidential. I'm picking up the final copies at the end of the week, so it's gonna be a surprise, even for the authors, until the official debut. We're setting up a table at the championship game. Give this one a look, though. I just need it back on Monday."

Mia gripped the hardcover tightly in her hands. Before, it was only a book. Now, it was a book containing *Bryce's* words. "Are you sure, Chloe?"

"Absolutely." She looked over her shoulder and whispered, "Bryce wanted you to read it first. That was his one condition for publishing his piece."

Stunned, Mia simply nodded. When she eventually found her voice, it was shaky. "Thank you, Chloe."

"Of course. Well, I'm gonna go check out the other tables. I think Mr. Phillips is selling fresh kettle corn and funnel cakes from his general store." Mia waved as her friend ran off, pulled by her unwavering appetite.

Still shell-shocked and clutching the blue book even tighter, Mia stood frozen in place. Finally, tearing her gaze from Bryce's printed name, she glanced back at her table. She couldn't stop herself from laughing out loud, seeing Bryce happily offering both treats *and* selfies to the masses of girls lining up. It was such a brilliant business strategy, she mentally smacked herself for not thinking of it before.

Deciding not to interrupt Bryce's adoring fan club, Mia made the most of her solitary opportunity and strolled over to a secluded spot behind the bleachers. She flopped onto the grass and opened the hard, glossy cover with trembling fingers. Mia had no idea why she was so nervous. But she remembered what it was like to get inside Bryce's head. Only now, she was reminded—this time—he had invited her. Taking a steadying breath within the muffled cocoon of the bleachers, she looked past his name and the intriguing title and was immediately drawn in.

Mia lost all sense of time while captured by the blue book. Only when the page ran out, and loud voices sounded in the distance, was she brought out of Bryce's spell. She knew he could write beautiful things about his mom, but this was beyond anything she could've imagined. Mia had no idea how to describe what she'd just read, or how it made her feel. His moving words had tugged at something she'd held in for so long but was only now able to let go.

With the voices growing closer, Mia finally shut the book. As she raised her chin to the breezy autumn sky, a stray tear fell from the corner of her eye, warming her chilled cheek. Nearby, three girls giggled and nibbled on brownies while huddled around the glow of their cell phones. Suddenly, hearing them mention Bryce's name, Mia wiped her damp cheek with the back of her hand and refocused her attention back to the day's main event. Dragging herself from behind the bleachers, she blinked away a few remaining tears, and hurried back to her table.

When she returned, Bryce was so inundated with customers, he could barely look up from their cash tin. With him fortunately preoccupied, Mia stuffed the blue book inside her backpack and attempted to regain her composure.

The crowd soon disbursed, and Bryce lifted his bright eyes in excitement. "Look, Mia!" he declared proudly, showing her several empty containers. "And ... you are officially out of gluten-free brownies."

"You're kidding?"

"Nope. Everyone kept asking where they could get more." Holding his head high, he pointed to the business cards. "And I told them."

"Very clever," she said with a subdued smile.

As their eyes held, Bryce's own smile faded. "Everything okay?"

She turned away from his analytical gaze. "Uh, yeah. Just a bit anxious for the final numbers on the sale."

A few minutes later, Mia was organizing the remaining containers, when a green lightsaber approached, attached to an adorable face. "Sir Eli!" she exclaimed, wrapping him in a hug. "Where's your brother?"

"Trying to keep up with this little guy," Zach said breathlessly, jogging up to their table. "Sorry, we're so late. Mom had an early shift this morning, and I needed to get this guy ready."

Mia walked around the table, meeting Zach for a hug. "No biggie. We have plenty left for our favorite knight."

Zach gave Bryce a quick fist bump. "Hey, man. Guess you've been recruited, huh?"

"No complaints," he said, bending down and slapping Eli a high-five.

Scanning the table, Zach grinned broadly. "Mia, this is incredible. You've definitely sold more than anyone else here. And these business cards are awesome. Your parents coming?"

"Yeah. My dad should be stopping by in a bit. And I sent some photos to my mom already. She seemed excited."

Handing Eli a cannoli cookie, Zach said, "Mia, my mom wanted to thank you for the lasagnas you brought over the other day. She's been working a ton of hours lately, so it's nice to have some delicious food in the freezer."

"Oh, it's no big deal. I was making one anyway," she said, flicking a glance toward Bryce. "Wait, Zach. I thought your mom was trying to reduce her hours."

He shrugged. "She keeps reminding me college is coming up fast. Can't always bank on football, so gotta save up."

Eli jumped up, tapping Mia with his lightsaber. "Queen Mia makes the best cookies in all the land," he announced, and they tried to contain their laughter.

"I concur, little buddy," Zach said, taking a cookie and pulling out his wallet.

Mia waved off his money. "Zach, you don't have to do that."

"No way, Mia. It's for a good cause." He pushed some bills toward her that she reluctantly accepted. "And these are amazing, as usual." Looking down at Eli, Zach offered his hand. "How about we go find our friends Harper and Chloe?"

Ignoring his hand, Eli ran up to Mia, tightly squeezing her. "I love you, Queen Mia," he said, leaving her heart to melt straight into the lush turf.

Kneeling beside him, she placed an almond biscotti into his tiny hand. "Here, Sir Eli. Your dad's favorite." He smiled, running back to his now glossy-eye brother. Zach gave her a wink as Eli dragged him off to the other side of the field.

"That was really nice, Mia," Bryce said.

She stood, wiping grass off her jeans. "I just wish I could do more." Watching Zach and Eli disappear into the crowd, she felt a pang in her chest and thought, *Maybe I can.*

Chapter 42

When Anthony DeSalvo made his way across the football field, sporting a sparkling white chef's jacket, his wild curly hair, and a radiant smile, he was bombarded by locals shaking his hand. Waving to his daughter, he beamed with pride. But, despite standing behind a table littered with empty containers, Mia's stomach contorted into several knots the moment she saw her dad. "*Buon giorno*, kiddo!" he cheered, outstretching his arms. "Wow. There's practically nothing left." She bit her lip, nervously playing with her hands and glancing back at Bryce.

"Mia's organized an amazing event, sir," he said to Anthony.

Mia's dad extended his hand to Bryce. "Nice to see you again, young man. Yes, Mia is really something special." Turning back to his flushed-faced daughter, he asked, "What did I hear about a cannoli cookie? Is that what you're calling our cannoli?"

"Um, actually, Papà," she started, taking a hard swallow. "It's this." She offered him one of the remaining cookies with bated breath.

After inspecting every intricate detail of the sandwich cookie, he eagerly tasted the creamy filling. Then, he took a generous bite, followed by another, finishing the cookie with a lick of his fingertips. Mia shifted her weight, squirming behind the table, unable to take the suspense. Finally, his lips curved into a wide grin. "This is delicious, Mia. Where'd it come from?"

"I made it," she croaked.

Seeing her hesitation, Bryce chimed in. "She made all of this, sir. Every one of the recipes she modified from her great-great-grandmother."

"Bryce!" she hissed, shooting him an annoyed look and a punch in the arm.

Taking in the table of goodies, Anthony ran his hand through his curls, then rubbed his bristly chin. "*Modified?* You mean, the book? But the cannoli? The flavors are spot-on."

"Um. I sort of found the bottle of *Fiori di Sicilia*," she said in a shaky voice. "The rest I ... reverse-engineered and *changed a bit*." Mia cringed, waiting for her dad's response, her stomach tightening with the pressure.

He gave her an incredulous look, then a smile, pulling her into a massive grizzly hug. "My brilliant Mia! Like her innovative nonna. Always coming up with new recipes. Looks like you made mine even better."

"What'd you mean? Isn't it Nonna's?"

"No, Mia. Well, not quite. When Antoinette opened the bakery, she had her own recipes. But she encouraged everyone to experiment like her. It was her love of innovation that's kept us in business for so long."

Mia frowned, scratching her head. "But... you were always so protective of the original recipes. And you didn't seem open to any changes."

"Yes. Well. You're right. I should listen to you and your mom more. Just like my brilliant daughter, I'm a bit stubborn." He playfully tousled Mia's hair. "But I think we can keep our bakery like Antoinette would have wanted while still being hip and modern."

"So, Wi-Fi and chai lattes, maybe?" she asked in a hopeful voice.

"What the heck is a chai latte?" he asked, and Mia and Bryce burst into hysterics.

"I'll get Chloe to fill you in, Papà. Apparently, she's an expert on the subject."

Anthony gave the table another once-over. "So, what else is new?"

"How about a dark chocolate cornetto?" she said, handing him a pastry. "Um, you may need a few to get through this." Mia lifted the thick, color-coded binder with a coy smile.

When the crowd had thinned and eaten through most of the tables, Harper came up to Mia, looking thrilled. "The turnout was off the charts! Look, boss. Preliminaries from everyone show we *surpassed* our fundraising goal." She excitedly tapped her pencil at the figures on her clipboard.

Barely able to believe her eyes, Mia beamed. "Fantastic, Harper! Because I think I have an idea to run by you."

Chapter 43

Mia was straightening the "Free Wi-Fi" sign in the bakery window as her mom dimmed the vintage overhead lights, casting a warm glow around the room. "Have you tried your dad's recent attempt at chai latte?" she asked, holding a cup over the counter.

Mia scrunched up her nose as she collected dishes from the tables, dropping them into a bin on the counter. "Nah. Think I'll wait until he's perfected it. The last four batches haven't been the best."

"Well, I'll leave it in case you change your mind. Although, I wholeheartedly agree." She gave the cup a wince, then reached over to turn off the espresso machine with a deep yawn.

"Mom, I got the rest of this. Go ahead and relax upstairs with Dad."

She pulled her daughter into a hug. "Thanks, sweetie. By the way, your dad said we sold out of cannoli cookies again *and* those gluten-free things you make."

"Yeah. He's excited about learning how to make the cookies, but I swear he breaks out in hives whenever I mention the phrase 'gluten-free.'"

"Ah. Don't we all?" her mom teased, trudging toward the stairs to their apartment. "Good night, sweetie."

Polishing a few smudges on the glass cases, Mia looked up and spotted a friendly face through the front windows. She raced to open the door, revealing a full face of dimples. "Hey, Bryce! Come in."

He glanced at her apron as he strolled inside. "You still working?"

"Yeah. My parents had a long day." Using her rag, she waved him over to the counter. "How was your last practice before the finals tomorrow?"

Bryce took a seat, setting his messenger bag on the counter. "Good. Zach brought Eli, so we had some fun playing catch after. I think I might stop by more; give Zach a hand at home."

"I'm sure they'd love that," she said, scrubbing the counter with her rag.

"You need any help?"

"Nah. I'm almost done. Hey, are you game to try some of my dad's new chai latte?" she asked, offering him the cup on the counter.

Looking inside, he made a grimace. "Yeah. Hard pass. Not really my thing."

"Don't blame you." She made a face at the cup, dumping its contents down the sink. "What about a pumpkin spice latte? I actually made this myself, so it's safer. I promise." With her head held high, Mia pushed another cup toward him. "And I used *real* spices and puree."

Taking a sip, Bryce smiled. "I'm not even a fan of those, but this is great. Pretty soon, there'll be no reason for people to go to Urban Coffee."

"Not sure Chloe would agree," she muttered, internally rolling her eyes.

"Speaking of bakery updates." He dug into his bag, pulling out his tablet. "I started working on this for you."

Mia hovered over the tablet as colorful pages of text and delicious photos filled the screen. "You did all this? When?"

"After you mentioned your old website. I checked it out and agree it looks pretty outdated. And the new photos are from the party the other night. Of course, you'll have to approve all the text and the menu. But I hope I got the history right, about your Nonna Antoinette."

"Actually." Mia tapped her finger to her lips as if something just occurred to her. Without a word, she whirled around and plucked a framed black and white photograph off the wall behind her. After quickly dusting it with her rag, she offered it to Bryce. "Maybe you could use this for one of the pages."

He examined the old photo, the edges wrinkled with age. Holding the faded frame up to the light, he squinted his eyes between it and Mia. "Wow. That's remarkable."

"What?" she asked, looking back at the frame with curious eyes.

Bryce pointed to the image of apron-wearing Antoinette, positioned behind the very counter where Mia now stood. Her eyes and smile were bright and cheerful, and her long, ebony locks were collected into a bun. "You look just like her."

Mia giggled, staring at the photograph as if it carried her back in time one hundred years. "I hear that a lot. But I haven't looked at this in a while." Finally, pulling herself from the image, she pushed it back toward Bryce. "So, feel free to scan it for the site. You're right about us having history on our side. And thanks. This is exactly what we need," she said, her gaze transfixed on the beautifully constructed pages. "I bet my dad is gonna love them."

Bryce carefully slid the frame and his tablet into his bag. "Well, that's a change of heart."

"Yeah, well, I think I learned not to underestimate my dad. And, speaking of which, maybe you shouldn't either," she said casually, resuming her counter scrubbing.

"Maybe. We'll see. But I did get him to agree to come to the game tomorrow."

"How?"

Shrugging, he said, "I think he's impressed enough that his son, the new quarterback, helped get the school to the championships. Even if it isn't Wellington."

"Well, I get why they'd want you back." She bowed her head and focused on the counter.

"I'm still working on it, Mia."

Lifting her gaze, she changed the subject. "Anyway, at least Ms. Marsh released you from your torturous sessions with your tutor." She gave him a teasing nudge with her elbow.

"Actually, I'm hoping my favorite tutor might still want to do some assignments together. Honestly, Mia, you're fantastic with math and science."

"Thanks. I think that could be arranged. And maybe we could make a deal. I could always use some help with my English papers. It just so happens I know an amazing writer."

"No kidding," he teased sarcastically.

"Yeah. I've even thought about starting a journal."

Bryce raised his eyebrows. "Hmm. Think you'd want to share?"

Mia shook her head vigorously. "Uh, no. I also learned it's best to keep those thoughts to yourself." She grabbed a fresh, clean rag and headed to the far end of the bakery, wiping down the rest of the tables. Bryce followed slowly, carrying his messenger bag.

"Um, Mia. There's something I've been meaning to talk to you about." As she turned to face him, he rocked back on his heels nervously, then revealed the infamous black and white composition book from the depths of his bag. "I think it's time you finished it."

When he pushed it toward her, she shuddered, waving it away. "No way, Bryce. That's yours. I should never have read a word of it."

He followed her as she started cleaning the front windows. "Mia, I *want* you to read it. You need to know how I really…Please take it." As she pushed it away again, he reiterated, "Please, Mia. I need you to see the whole picture."

She blew out an exasperated sigh, reluctantly taking the journal and holding it awkwardly in her hands. "I'll think about it, okay?"

Nodding, Bryce closed the distance between them. He hesitated, then tucked a stray wisp of hair behind her ear with a featherweight touch of his fingertip. A flutter of butterflies enveloped Mia, bringing her gaze to the floor as his soft touch lingered on her temple.

"I should go," he said quietly. "Gotta get ready for tomorrow." They ambled side-by-side toward the door, neither in a hurry to depart.

"Good luck at the game. And be careful, okay?" She raised her eyes to meet his and slowly reached for the door handle. "Um, Bryce. You're coming back here tomorrow for the party, right?"

"Of course. I wouldn't miss it." As he angled close to her in the threshold, his breath warmed her cheek to a rosy red. Leaning in farther, his lips nearly brushed her ear. "Sweet dreams, Mia," he said, his voice barely a whisper, before walking out with a *jingle*. Watching Bryce disappear into the darkness, she was finally able to catch her breath.

Later, passing by the snores of her parents conked out in front of the TV, Mia tiptoed to her room and closed the door. Stretching out on her bed, she focused on the composition book, now sitting heavy in her hands. As she attempted to open the cover, she shuddered yet again and slammed it closed. Mia mentally scolded herself for taking it back. Why would she want to reopen that wound?

With another exasperated sigh, she tucked herself beneath her comforter, shoving the book under a tall pile of pillows. Resting against it, she hoped to smother its brutally honest words. But, amid the quiet confines of her darkened room, the journal's harsh revelations echoed in her head. Mia squeezed her eyes shut and flipped over restlessly.

Even hours later, when she eventually drifted off to sleep, the sting and weight of Bryce's words rested painfully on her mind and her chest.

Chapter 44

When Mia awoke the next morning, Bryce's journal was still burning a hole through her pillow. No matter how hard she tried, she couldn't bring herself to open it. What if the next page was worse than the one before it? Mustering up enough courage to reach for it again, her hand froze on its cover. With a *groan*, she hid it back under her pillows. Finally, throwing off her comforter in frustration, she heaved herself out of bed.

As she hurried down the stairs to the bakery, her long ponytail (tied with a blue and gold ribbon to match her sweatshirt) swung enthusiastically back and forth. Rushing toward the kitchen to grab her apron like every other morning, Mia abruptly stopped in her tracks. She rubbed her eyes, unable to believe them. A quick glance at her watch revealed it was barely 9 a.m., and yet, it appeared to her untrusting eyes that the bakery was absolutely overflowing. Walking farther into the space, she saw her mom behind the counter, her hands full with an endless line of hungry customers.

Mia's feet were still cemented to the floor when her mom turned to refill a coffee cup with fresh brew. "Morning, sweetie. Would you mind getting Mrs. Rossi's usual order? She's been so patiently waiting."

Her fog lifting, Mia ran into the kitchen for her apron. She found her dad with a piping bag in his hand, happily humming along as he swiftly filled a large tray of cannoli. Looking up, he ran to his daughter and hugged her close. "Good morning, Mia. What a wonderful day it is!"

"Um, yeah. Papà, what's with all the people out front?" she asked, reaching for her apron. But he just gave her a wink and continued humming and filling cannoli shells.

Moments later, Mia was still in a daze, weaving her way through lively patrons, enjoying cookies, pastries, and other baked delicacies with their coffees. When she located Mrs. Rossi's table, the older woman greeted her with a lovely smile and reached for a strand of her long ponytail. "So pretty, Mia. You look adorable in your blue and gold. What's the occasion?"

Mia passed her the steaming cup of cappuccino and plate of biscotti. "My school made it to the State Championship in football. We're going to the final game this afternoon. I have some great friends on the team."

Mrs. Rossi took a sip from her coffee. "Well, wish them the best of luck. My husband used to play football years ago."

Mia's eyes lit up as she sat down beside her. "Really?" she asked, hunched forward with interest.

Rummaging through her purse, Mrs. Rossi unearthed a tattered black and white photo of an attractive man with an athletic build wearing a vintage football uniform. He lunged at the camera while cradling an old football and flashing his biggest toothy grin.

"He was so handsome," Mia said, staring at the photo.

"Yes, he was. State Champions, too. He so loved being the quarterback." She looked longingly past Mia into the distance, draining her coffee cup.

"Would you like me to bring you anything else, Mrs. Rossi?"

Suddenly, Mia's dad swung out of the kitchen, holding a white box tied with a red and white bow. "Sophia! These are freshly filled, just for you." He handed her the box to her delight. "And I even added a few cannoli cookies Mia baked. They're our new best sellers."

"Oh, how wonderful! *Grazie!*" she said with a wink. As he ran back into the kitchen, she whispered to Mia, "Dear, you think you could make me one of those new pumpkin spice lattes? So perfect for this chilly fall weather." Mia smiled, walking away with a chuckle.

When she returned with the latte, Mrs. Rossi was deeply engrossed in her cell phone. "Oh, thank you, dear. I love being able to get online and see what my great-grandchildren are up to." Holding up her phone and taking a photo of the latte, she added, "It's like I'm sharing my breakfast with them." Then, Mrs. Rossi lifted the cup of fresh, spiced pumpkin goodness to her nose and inhaled deeply. "Ooh. It even smells like fall!" Mia beamed, feeling a sense of pride surge through her.

A couple of hours later, Mia was grateful when the door jingled, revealing Harper and Chloe's astonished faces. Waving them over to the counter through the chaos, she threw them an exasperated look.

"What the heck happened in here?" Harper asked, taking in the scene. "We could barely get through the door."

Mia collapsed over the counter and dropped her head in her hands. "You know the saying, 'be careful what you wish for?' Well, I'm totally living it."

"Are you gonna be able to get away for the game?" Chloe asked. She instantly lost interest in her answer, eyeing the full case of cookies and pastries and starting to drool.

"Yeah. My mom said I can leave whenever. Honestly, I think my parents are just thrilled by the turnout. It's been increasing all week, but this is a madhouse."

"So, you ready to face the Springdale Cougars? You know, State Champs five years running?" Harper asked, pulling Chloe from the case.

Mia eagerly ripped off her apron, replacing it with her jacket from the coat stand. "Yup. Let's do this!" She sprinted for the door with her bike helmet and a wave to her mom.

After the girls parked their bikes, amid the crunchy, spent leaves of a large oak, they made their way over to the already-bustling field. "Wow! This place must be twice the size of our stadium. And that grass looks as good as AstroTurf," Harper gushed, referring to the pristinely lined and lush football field, flanked by tall, shiny bleachers. Even at this early hour, they were swiftly filling up with opposite ends of blue and gold and red and black.

"At least it was a short ride this time. Nice to finally get a game closer to home," Mia said, eyeing the elaborate LED scoreboard, the size of a small nation.

"Yeah. Our *one* advantage," Harper moaned. "I hear these guys are ruthless."

Walking past the packed concession stand, Chloe halted, contemplating the large menu hanging overhead. "Hmm. I'm thinking nachos, definitely."

"Chloe, it's not even noon yet," Harper said, attempting to drag her away.

Pulling free, Chloe secured a place in line. "Whatever, Harper. You kept me from the biscotti, so this is what you get."

Leaving Chloe to own devices, Harper pointed to the field. "Look. The guys are warming up. I'll say hi, then grab us some seats. You coming, Mia?"

"Um. Yeah. In a minute." Drawing in the refreshing autumn air, Mia relaxed over the fence surrounding the field as both teams stretched and worked on agility drills. She cringed at the Springdale players' muscular builds and intense focus, especially their number 3 spry quarterback. *These guys mean business,* she thought.

As she shifted her attention to the Eagles' side, Logan cheerfully waved to Harper in the distance, then concentrated on kicking several balls through the towering goalposts. Mia crept closer to the sidelines and finally spotted Zach and Bryce chatting with Coach Warner. With a quick wave and a smile through his facemask, Zach continued his conversation. To her surprise, Bryce dismissed himself and jogged toward her, cradling his shiny gold helmet.

"Hey, Mia." He flashed full dimples, and she felt her heart skip around a little.

"That definitely looks better without the mud," she teased, pointing to his impeccably clean gold number 5.

"I know, right? At least it's a nice, dry field today." He cocked his head toward the already-brimming stands. "Good turnout, too."

Mia raised her gaze to the cloudless deep blue sky. "Yeah. The warm weather probably helps." Pointing out Springdale's number 3, she made a scowl. "Any thoughts on your competition?"

"Yeah, actually. Ran into Kyle a few times when I was playing for Wellington. Summer football camp. No question, he's earned the top quarterback spot."

"Are you nervous?" she asked. "Um, not to put on the pressure or anything."

Bryce ran his fingers through his slightly damp waves. "Nah. I'm good. I know today's important." He cut his eyes to the stands. "But this is what we practice for, so," he said with a shrug.

Mia kicked around some grass at her feet. "I wish I could be as calm."

"What'd you mean?" Leaning toward her, he squinted against the dazzling sun.

"I guess I'm a little nervous about halftime. The presentation. Silly, huh?"

"Mia, it's gonna be perfect, like everything you do." He lightly touched the tip of her ponytail as his eyes locked on hers.

"Thanks," she said, feeling her face heat up to the same shade as her opponents' jerseys. "Um, I should probably let you get back to your warm-ups."

As she started to walk away, Bryce yelled back, "Mia, did you get a chance to finish—?" but was interrupted by Coach Warner's shrill whistle, calling in the huddle.

"Good luck!" she shouted, heading for the bleachers and leaving Bryce mid-sentence.

Chapter 45

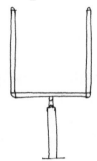

With only three minutes left in the first quarter, Mia had no clue how her Eagles had managed to restrict the Cougars to only one trip to the end zone. This was especially true, considering her opponents had an annoying habit of winning their games by double digits. It was still a 0-7 game when Bryce made another impressive appearance on the field. Although they had yet to add any points to the board, his offensive line looked superb against Springdale's fantastic defense, making it close to the end zone several times. But, while the Eagles' opponents certainly weren't small players, their speed was their real weapon.

Mia was fidgeting in her seat, nervously chewing on her fingernails, when Chloe left for a second jaunt to the concession stands, claiming it "calmed her nerves." As Mia's eyes moved from Bryce to the dwindling numbers on the clock, she was silently praying GW would get at least *something* on the scoreboard before the end of the quarter.

Thankfully, Bryce's next pass sailed high over the Cougars' defense and landed easily in the hands of his intended receiver for a well-executed first down. With only a few yards to the goal line, Bryce directed a tight spiral straight to a surprisingly open Zach in the end zone, earning them their first points of the game. Mia blew out a sigh of relief as Logan looked in top form, tying things up between the goalposts.

But, by the middle of the second quarter, things weren't looking so rosy. When Chloe returned with a king-sized basket of cheesy curly fries, the Cougars and their ridiculously accurate quarterback were on a roll, scoring two more touchdowns. While Mia grumbled, "This is a disaster," with her head in her hands, the other side of the stadium cheered loudly when their no-nonsense kicker knocked in another flawless extra point.

Harper patted her on the shoulder. "At least it's almost halftime, and we'll get a break from it."

Bryce must have been tired of this disaster of a game as well because the next time he marched up to the line of scrimmage, it was with a fresh look of determination in his eyes. The result was his first pass flying straight to Zach for an easy first down. The next play wasn't quite as straightforward. When Bryce broke forward to rush, the Cougars' speed tested his own striking agility. "Come on, Bryce," Mia muttered, watching him weave flawlessly around several players. Sprinting forward like a cannonball, he earned the Eagles another first down. But one look at Bryce bent over and gasping for breath, and it was clear all of this was putting quite a strain on their star quarterback.

Mia was still homed in on the game when Harper tugged on her sweatshirt, pointing to the clock on the field. "It's time. Dr. Alexander wants us out there extra early."

Leaving the comforting confines of the bleachers for the hectic sidelines, Mia's stomach dropped several notches. She reached into her rear jeans' pocket and pulled out some notecards, for a quick refresher. But her gaze was drawn back to the field and the Cougars' bright red uniforms that seemed to illuminate their fierce expressions. She didn't know what was more terrifying, the indomitable glint in her opponents' eyes or her own impending appearance on the field. "Mia, you're gonna be great. Trust me, he'll love it," Harper whispered, squeezing her arm.

"I hope so," she said tentatively, shifting her focus between the notecards and the intense game around her.

With the clock winding down to less than two minutes in the half, Bryce's patience and energy were thinning, and he opted to throw the ball to the far end zone, instead of an easier pass a few yards away. It was a gutsy move and almost appeared successful. That is, until a red number 50 jersey, built like a combination of the Incredible Hulk and a refrigerator, bolted for the ball, knocking it out of the Eagles' hands.

Suddenly, out of the corner of Mia's eye, she saw the airborne football spinning toward her. Although her reflexes told her to go for the ball, she knew what always followed it. Pushing Harper out of the way, she jumped back just in time for Number 50 to land at her feet with a loud *thud* and a gasp from the crowd. Mia's breathing resumed as the player jumped up, offering a quick, "Sorry," then a charming wink at Harper.

"Geez. That was close," Harper said in a shaky voice.

"You're telling me," Mia replied, waiting for her heart rate to slow. She glanced over at Bryce and Zach, who looked as relieved. "He almost intercepted our ball!"

"I was kinda referring to him almost tackling you. But at least he was cute." Harper let out a high-pitched giggle, and Mia rolled her eyes, then returned them to her notecards.

Now, with less than a minute to go on the clock, Bryce's face showed frustration. He hurled the ball with a *grunt*, way over the Cougars' heads and across the field to his farthest wide receiver. Collapsing to his knees in exhaustion, relief appeared to wash over him when his deep pass was caught just across the line. After Logan's spot-on kick, it was a one-possession, 14-21 game, as GW closed in on Springdale's lead at the end of the first half.

While the players jogged off to the locker room for some inspirational speeches, the marching bands and dance teams took over the field for a couple of quick performances. Mia paced nervously along the sidelines until she saw the shimmer of gold helmets reappear from across the stadium.

When GW's principal, Dr. Olivia Alexander, carried a microphone to a platform set up on the 50-yard line, she received rousing applause. "Good afternoon! What a beautiful day for a fantastic championship game!" she announced to the pumped crowd. "I am so proud to introduce a well-respected member of our student body at George Washington High, who has a wonderful announcement to make to our close community. Please give a warm greeting to GW's Freshman Class President, Mia DeSalvo!"

When Mia crossed the turf, bathed in brilliant sunlight, she was shaking from head to toe. While she usually loved public speaking, especially in front of her classmates, she knew this wasn't just a simple fundraising speech. It was far more important than that. "Good luck," Dr. Alexander whispered to Mia, who couldn't help but think she was going to need it. She accepted the mic from her animated principal and flashed her biggest smile as the crowd continued to cheer. With one final glance at her notes, she tucked them inside the pocket of her sweatshirt, preferring to speak from the heart.

"Thank you, Dr. Alexander, for allowing us to make this special presentation," she started, her voice quivering. Pausing, she sucked in a deep calming breath before continuing, stronger this time. "As many of you know, one of the highlights of our GW experience is giving back to the community. For our charity project this semester, we chose to raise much-needed funds for our local food bank. While we had many events to help meet our goal, our recent bake sale really put us over the top." She waited as massive applause ensued. Dr. Alexander waved in the food bank representative, Andrea Luca, who approached the field and sincerely thanked Mia with a grateful embrace.

Next, Mia introduced their "amazing fundraising chair." With bright eyes, Harper announced into the mic, "We are thrilled to help such an important part of the community. Thanks to everyone's love of sugar, this year's fundraiser was a huge success!" Amid laughter and cheers, Harper waited a few beats to build up the suspense, her face now a mixture of giddy and proud. "And, because of your generosity, we not only met our goal but exceeded it. In fact, we more than *doubled* it." As the stadium overflowed with deafening cheers, Harper presented a life-sized check to an ecstatic Ms. Luca, who completely ignored her handshake and, instead, engulfed her in a hug. After a few chuckles, she passed the mic and the presentation back to Mia.

Cutting her eyes at Zach, who was fully engrossed in the scene on the 50-yard line, Mia's heart was in her throat. Beside him stood Bryce, giving her his undivided attention with a gleaming dimpled grin. Meeting his gaze, Mia immediately felt more at ease as she lifted her mic. "Because of the unanticipated success of our fundraising event, we choose to use the extra funds to help another wonderful cause. So, after consultation with Ms. Luca and the student body, we decided to start an annual scholarship..." She paused, her mouth bone-dry as she took a steadying breath. "...in the name of a very special GW alumnus, former All-State Football Champ and decorated Army Veteran: *the late Captain Zachary Redding Sr.*"

Mia took a hard swallow and bit her lower lip, trying to assess Zach's stoic facial expression from across the field. When she lifted her mic the final time, her voice was once again quivering but, this time, with emotion. "And the student council could think of no better first recipient than his son, GW Eagles' amazing number 44 sophomore running back, *Zach Redding Jr.*"

Chapter 46

Zach's mouth dropped open when Mia announced his name. He remained frozen on the sidelines until Bryce pushed him forward with the rest of the team's help, who applauded and cheered enthusiastically. Coach Warner jumped into the crowd and happily guided Lauryl and Eli (lightsaber in hand) to the field for the surprise presentation.

When Zach finally made his way up to Mia on the platform, their eyes held for a long moment. She gave him a shy smile and a shrug as he wiped his damp cheeks with the sleeve of his jersey. "Thank you so much, Mia," he said softly, affectionately pulling her into his trembling arms. Lauryl joined them, hugging both Mia and little Eli close to her. With most of the stadium fighting back tears, Mia presented a framed certificate and a check to a still-shocked Zach.

After several posed photographs, a few reporters from local newspapers grabbed the emotional running back for some brief words before Coach Warner called in a huddle to start the second half. Dr. Alexander walked off the field with Lauryl, cheerfully chatting away while Sir Eli clung to his mom's blue and gold sweatshirt. Mia and Harper waved to Zach as they strolled over to the concession stand for a well-deserved snack.

When they arrived, members of the literary magazine editorial board were staffing a large table, brimming with tall stacks of blue hardcovers. Mia figured it was Chloe's clever idea to position the table right beside the concessions. Regardless, based upon the long line now forming, the blue books were selling like hotcakes (or at least as well as the hot dog Chloe was currently holding in her hand). "Hey, guys! Fantastic speeches," she said to Mia and Harper as she left the table. "And Zach looked absolutely floored!"

"Thank goodness," Mia said, expelling a held breath. "Now, if we could only get ahead in this game."

"Seriously," Harper agreed. Taking a longing look at Chloe's half-consumed snack, she eyed the concession stand menu. "Maybe you're on to something, Chloe, with the food."

Munching on her hot dog, she replied. "I know, right?"

Mia gestured toward the queue forming at Chloe's table, appearing longer with each passing second. "So, how are sales going? I mean, things look brisk."

"It's been awesome! Fingers crossed we sell out by the end of the game," she said, polishing off her hot dog. "Oh, wait, Mia. Hold on." Chloe smacked her forehead, racing back to the table. She grabbed a copy from one of the quickly dissolving stacks and presented it to Mia. "Sorry. Gotta give you your final copy before there's a riot."

"Yeah. It's starting to look like Christmas Eve at the Toy-A-Rama." Mia laughed and ran the book over to her bike basket.

Mia and Harper were leaving the concessions with their oversized pretzels when the stadium's blue and gold side erupted into booming cheers. "Yes! We're tied!" Harper exclaimed, pointing her mustard packet at the illuminated scoreboard.

"See!" Chloe said, now lugging a giant bucket of buttery popcorn. "The food thing totally works."

Chloe wandered off to share her popcorn with Abbie and the cheerleaders while Mia and Harper returned to the stands. But, when Mia passed the Eagles' benches, she was stopped in her tracks. As her last bite of pretzel barely slid down, she couldn't tear her eyes from a beaming gentleman, proudly patting Bryce on the back. Apparently, he had seen the last fantastic touchdown, flawlessly executed by their star quarterback. But what *didn't* impress Mia was what he was wearing. His sweatshirt had the all-too-familiar crest with a large burgundy "W" in the center. And, when she got an even better view of his ball cap, her heart started pounding—at the big block letters spelling out… "Wellington Prep Football."

Chapter 47

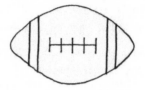

Slipping into her seat, Mia's stomach turned. Her gaze traveled to her hand and her now unappealing snack. "You want this?" she asked Harper, pushing her half-eaten pretzel toward her.

"Sure," she answered with a shrug. "It worked for one touchdown. Can't hurt to keep trying."

When Chloe returned with an empty bucket of popcorn, Mia was slumped over in the bleachers, her chin cupped in her hand, having lost all interest in the game. Suddenly, with one swift bullet of a pass, the Cougars landed in the end zone, leading the Eagles, again. Mia rolled her eyes at the scoreboard as Chloe squeezed in between her and Harper. "What did I miss?"

"Nothing good," Harper whined, making a face at Chloe's empty popcorn bucket. She rose to her feet and added, "I'm gonna get something else to eat. This is all too depressing."

When she left, Chloe whispered to Mia, "So, we thought we might try to convince Bryce to join the editorial board for the spring edition of the magazine. What do you think?"

Taken aback, Mia was instantly brought out of her stupor. "Chloe, I don't know."

"Well, I figured you could talk to him about it. He totally listens to you, obvi."

Mia cringed, sliding a glance at the Wellington sweatshirt and then back to Chloe. "I'm not so sure that's true."

"Sure, it is. Give it some thought. You know he'd be awesome."

Pulling herself from the uncomfortable conversation, Mia directed her gaze back to the field as the Eagles tried to do anything to keep up with the impressive Cougars. When Bryce caught his next snap, almost 60 yards short of the goal, she watched with disinterested eyes. With no receiver in sight, he shot forward to rush, tightly cradling the ball. There was no question Bryce was an incredible sprinter, even against the *Usain Bolt efforts* by the Cougars. But, as Mia's eyes followed him down the field, they shifted to a red uniform, closing in on him, *rapidly*. And, with Bryce's sights set on the goal line, he seemed completely oblivious to what was going on behind him. Mia sat up straight, her attention now grabbed. When the giant red uniform appeared mere steps away, she sprang from her seat. Cupping her hands around her mouth, she yelled, "Bryce! Behind you!"

Whether by chance or Mia's booming voice, Bryce glanced behind him, just in time to leap out of the red uniform's reach, narrowly avoiding a hard tackle. Seemingly proud of himself, he sped up, weaving around several other players and finally *vaulting over* Number 50, like something out of a gravity-defying ninja movie. He made it to the end zone and collapsed to his knees, ending the third quarter as everyone in the stands simply stared, dumbstruck.

"OMG! Did Bryce actually just do that?" Harper screamed, through the loud cheers of blue and gold, nearly dropping her tray of nachos.

Mia crumpled into her seat, hearing her heart still thrashing in her chest. "That was way too close." She cut a glance at Harper's nachos, trying to hide her grimace as her friends eagerly dug in. "Argh! I can't take this stress."

"I know," Harper said between crunches. "Next time, definitely bring the baked goods."

When the Cougars' offense took over at the beginning of the fourth quarter, Bryce was still catching his breath along the sidelines. This crazy game of cat and mouse between two impressive quarterbacks clearly wasn't only affecting Bryce. As the Cougars lined up for their first possession of the quarter, their normally-stealth number 3 looked fatigued and confused, holding on to the ball for far too long. His indecisiveness proved costly, allowing the Eagles' phenomenal defense to take advantage, sacking him in one swift move.

"Ouch," Harper said, cringing behind her nachos. "That had to hurt. Isn't Kyle the top high school quarterback in the state?"

"Not anymore," Chloe said cheerfully, stealing the last of her friend's nachos.

Unfortunately, for the Cougars, that wasn't the last of it. With one more sack and two incomplete passes, the Eagles' defense was certainly showing them "who's boss." As the offense returned to the field, Bryce got little time to recuperate. Mia kept a keen eye on the giant clock running down, hoping *anyone* would score at this point in regulation. The last thing any of them could stomach was an overtime situation.

Balancing his intense focus between the clock and his coach, Bryce threw two more fantastic passes, strategically moving the team toward the goal. After the next snap, with his hands tightly gripping the ball, Bryce wound back as if in slow motion. Behind his facemask, his eyes moved between a free path to rush or a riskier long pass to Zach, mere inches from the end zone. Taking a few beats to assess his choices, he smiled at Zach and gunned the ball straight for him. Mia and the entire GW bleachers stood and held their collective breath as Zach jumped up and caught the ball, landing in the heart of the end zone. He hopped up and down, spiking the football on the turf, and the Eagles' side of the stadium went wild. When Logan made a brilliant kick to seal their lead to 7, Zach and Bryce slapped him on the back and banged helmets, celebrating on the sidelines.

"I can't believe this is happening!" Harper squealed in delight.

Mia couldn't keep herself from beaming. "I know. GW hasn't been this good in years. Who knew this was even possible?"

Harper nodded toward the sidelines. "Well, you know it's because of your buddy Bryce. He and Zach are like a dream team now."

Mia sneaked a peek at Bryce and Zach, grinning and doing one of those male-bonding-handshake things. She had to admit Harper was right. Her heart sank at the thought of the "dream team" being broken up by the likes of Wellington.

With only a few seconds left in the State Championship Final between the George Washington Eagles and the Springdale Cougars, every single body in the stadium was on its feet. Mia knew this game had been a showcase of the talented quarterbacks. Now, she hoped the experienced GW defense could hold their own for just one more play.

Keeping her eyes strictly on the dwindling clock, Mia heard a whistle, then the snap fly into Number 3's hands. Nervously lifting her gaze, her heart started to race. Kyle's eyes swept the field and finally rested on an open receiver, comfortably waiting in the end zone. Launching a Hail Mary pass across the emerald field and high into the cornflower-blue sky, Kyle looked as uncertain as the rest of the stadium. Mia covered her face and crumbled into her seat... until she heard the *roar* of the crowd around her.

"OMG! We intercepted it! Mia, we won!" Harper screamed, jumping up and down as Mia sat motionless in disbelief.

Within seconds, hundreds of jubilant fans spilled blue and gold onto the field. Chloe and Abbie dragged everyone toward the tight cluster of raised gold helmets, their sides adorned with majestic eagles. The girls were in hysterics, watching gallons of green Gatorade being dropped on Coach Warner. Then, the team hoisted up their dripping-wet coach high in victory, chanting the GW Eagles Fight Song.

As Mia's friends danced around the chaotic and packed stadium, it was clear how difficult it would be to get anywhere near Zach, Logan, or even Bryce. Pushing through the mosh pit, formerly known as the student section, Mia felt a tap on her shoulder. She spun around to an elated Zach, fully soaked in green liquid. "Is that apple?" she joked, wrinkling her nose at his uniform.

"You bet!" He pulled her into his drenched jersey, lifting her off the ground.

"Congratulations, Zach," she said, giggling as he squeezed her tightly. "But you're making me all sticky!"

"Mia! This seriously was the best day ever! Thank you so much!" He swung her around a few times, then set her gently on the ground.

"You're welcome. But you're the one who won the game."

As his face suddenly grew more solemn, Zach tilted his chin up to the sun's brilliant rays, illuminating the picture-perfect sky. "We all did. For my dad."

The hair on Mia's neck prickled as she looked above. "Yeah. For your dad."

Zach's grin returned as he ran off, spreading his Gatorade love everywhere he went. Mia scanned the rest of the field and spotted Bryce's dad, patting him on the back. Pushing forward through the thick crowd, she knew she needed to congratulate their star quarterback. But, moving only a few paces, she froze. Squinting through the chaos, she felt her stomach nosedive, catching Bryce and his dad enthusiastically shaking hands with the gentleman in the Wellington sweatshirt.

No longer feeling the thrill of victory, Mia pivoted on the spot, weaving through the crowd toward the edge of the field. Along the way, she passed Harper, chatting with Logan and one of the Cougars on the opposite end of the field. Not interested in a chat, she picked up her pace until a hand rested gently on her shoulder. Spinning around, Mia was face-to-face with a set of remarkable hazel eyes, now glossy and reflecting the green of the surrounding field and the blue of the autumn sky above.

Chapter 48

H ey, Mia," Bryce said softly as he reached for a quick hug. She gave him a genuine but subdued smile. "Congratulations." Then, Mia did a double take. Except for his damp waves, curled around his ears and matted down from his helmet, Bryce looked almost pristine. Taking in his Gatorade-free appearance, she said, "Wait. How'd you manage to stay dry?"

"Thanks. And it helps to be fast," he joked. Mia couldn't stop herself from grinning wider.

Pointing to the opposite end of the field, she said, "Good to see your dad here. He must be so proud."

"Yeah. Everyone is pretty stoked. Wanna come say hi?"

She shook her head, starting to back away. The last thing she wanted to witness was a Wellington reunion. "No, thanks. I probably should get going. Gotta help set up for the party."

"Um, Mia. Think you could stay a little longer? We have an announcement to make, and I'd really like you to hear it. Please." Their eyes locked for a beat, and Mia simply nodded.

As she walked away, a hollow feeling sat deep in her gut. Pushing through the chaos and arriving at the edge of the field, she was grateful to run into Harper. Mia had zero interest in sticking around to hear Bryce announce his return to Wellington.

"You ready to go? I need to get back to the bakery," she said hurriedly to her friend.

"Sure. But people are saying they're gonna make a big announcement during the trophy presentation." Harper pointed to the field, where the platform stage was again pulled out. A green-soaked Coach Warner pushed through the crowd, joyfully accepting the gigantic, gilded trophy. Before passing it to the players and fans below, he hoisted it high up into the air, revealing a gold football, glistening in the bright sun.

Turning from the scene, Mia sighed. "Yeah. Bryce wanted me to stay for it."

Harper paused, pensive for a moment. "Then maybe we should. Come on." She dragged a reluctant Mia back toward the field.

Meanwhile, Coach Warner grabbed the microphone and addressed the crowd. "Thanks for coming to celebrate GW's first State Championship win in years!" His thunderous voice echoed throughout the rowdy field of blue and gold. "Despite such a memorable season, we know all good things must eventually come to an end. This fall, we were blessed to have an impressive young man transfer to our school and help bring us this victory. Now, he has something important to share with you all. Please give it up for Bryce Fitzgerald, our fantastic quarterback and MVP!"

Mia shifted her weight uncomfortably on the edge of the field, barely able to watch as Bryce took center stage to overwhelming applause. "Thanks, Coach," he started. The moment she heard Bryce's voice, she couldn't help but lift her gaze to the sun-drenched platform. "When I came to GW, I never could have imagined meeting such amazing teammates and friends." He paused, fist bumping Zach and Logan beside him. "Even with an extended season, I wish it could last forever. But Coach is right. This had to end eventually." He paused again, taking in the crowd and the moment. "When Zach asked me to wear his dad's number 5, I wasn't fully aware of its significance." Bryce looked over at Zach, who sniffled with his head bowed. "Captain Redding was a hero, and I've been absolutely honored to wear his number for even this short time at GW. I just hope I did it justice."

Zach patted him on the back while everyone cheered loudly for their MVP. Then, Bryce relinquished his mic to his proud coach, who continued, "Tonight, we have invited Thomas Miller, Bryce's former coach at Wellington Prep, to join in a special announcement."

Turning away from the field, Mia concentrated on counting the blades of grass at her feet. When she started to walk off again, Harper called after her, "Mia, wait! Coach is about to give the big announcement."

Mia paused, hearing her heart practically beating out of her chest. She held her breath and shut her eyes, waiting for Coach Warner to continue. "We are so excited to announce that Bryce will don the prestigious number 5, once again, when he plays for George Washington High next year!"

Wondering if her ears were deceiving her, Mia whipped around to face the field. Her mouth fell open as she watched Bryce's old coach slap him on the back. After shaking hands, Bryce gifted him a blue and gold GW Eagles cap. When Coach Miller enthusiastically swapped it with his own Wellington one, the fans went crazy.

Harper joined in the enthusiastic applause. "This is awesome, right?" But her friend didn't answer her. She simply stared. "You okay, Mia?"

"I'm just surprised...and confused." She rubbed her forehead, finally stumbling off the field. "I figured this was about him being sucked back into Wellington. Why's he staying?"

"Boss, I think you should know something."

Reaching her bike under the swaying limbs of the bare oak, Mia dug out her helmet from the basket. She suppressed a *groan* at the blue book sitting underneath. "I'm not in the mood for another revelation tonight, Harper. I just want to get home."

"Mia, this is important." She paused, drawing in a deep breath. "We definitely exceeded our fundraising goal with the bake sale. But something else brought us *way* over."

"What?"

"Bryce's dad's donation."

Mia's eyes got huge. "Harper, what are you talking about?"

She heaved a heavy sigh. "Well, it was supposed to be anonymous. That's how Bryce wanted it. After the sale, he came up to me and asked if there was anything he could do, especially knowing how important the food bank was to you. And then, I kinda spilled the beans about your other idea."

"Harper, you didn't!"

"I had to, Mia. You should have seen the sincere look on his face. And, when I told him you wanted to do a scholarship in Zach's dad's name, he was so on board."

Mia squinted at the distant field, still able to make out Bryce and Mr. Fitzgerald on the platform. "But how'd he get his *dad* on board?"

"That, I don't know. All I know is, he wanted to do whatever he could for the people who've done so much for him since he started at GW."

Mia slowly slid on her helmet. "He said that?"

"Yeah, boss. I think GW means more to him than you thought. And, by GW, I also mean ..." She trailed off, strapping on her own helmet. But her words were lost in the void as Mia vigorously pedaled away, still in a state of shock.

Chapter 49

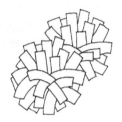

They biked to the bakery in complete silence, lost in thought. When Harper strolled through the door with Mia dragging behind, the final patrons of the day were finishing their coffees and cookies. Mia's mom greeted them from atop a ladder, hanging blue and gold balloons around a glittery banner that read, "Congratulations GW Eagles." "Hey, girls. Everyone's been coming in, sharing the fantastic news." She climbed down and offered some hugs. "Are you feeling okay, sweetie?" she asked, when her daughter barely looked up from the floor.

"Yeah, Mom. Just tired from the long day. And the field was crazy afterward." Wishing to change the subject, she said, "I'll go in the back and get the food ready. The hungry crowd should be filing in soon."

"I can help with the sign and balloons," Harper offered cheerfully, throwing Mia a sympathetic eye.

Mia's mom smiled. "Thank you, Harper." As her daughter breezed by, she called out, "Mia, your dad is cleaning up upstairs. He wanted to look nice for your party."

Bursting through the kitchen door, Mia was grateful for the long-awaited solitude. She slumped against the wall and threw the blue book onto the stainless countertop, trying to remember when things weren't quite so complicated.

With a few minutes to decompress, she came out in much better spirits. Holding a tray of treats, she approached Harper, talking with a large guy, outfitted only in red and black. Pausing her conversation, Harper said, "Mia! Let me introduce you. This is Chase."

"Wait. Aren't you the guy from Springdale who almost ran me over earlier?" Mia shot him a critical eye, setting down her tray. "And *almost* stole our ball."

Looking sheepish, he answered, "Uh, yeah. So sorry about that. Both things, actually."

"Chase is transferring to GW High next year," Harper said. Leaning in to Mia's ear, she whispered, "Cute, right, boss?"

"Yeah. I'll bet Logan doesn't think so," she hissed at her. Ignoring his cuteness factor, she focused on his muscular physique and strong arms. "I guess he'd be helpful in our scrimmage games. We need some decent defense."

Harper's eyes lit up. "Yeah. Totally."

Turning to Chase, Mia joked, "From Springdale to GW, huh? Well, at least that explains you crashing the party." She pointed to her tray. "Help yourself. These are cannoli cookies. The muffins are sugar-free. And these are gluten-free brownies."

His eyes brightened as he grabbed a brownie. "Thanks! I've totally been trying the Keto thing, so this is perfect."

Mia was shaking her head to herself when the door opened to a familiar face. "Sal!" she exclaimed, rushing over with her tray of goodies.

Sal gave her a side hug around her tray. "Miss Mia, do you remember my lovely wife, Elaine?"

"Of course. Great to see you, again. It's been a while."

Elaine flashed Mia a friendly smile. "I know. Poor Sal here's been busy at SkyView. But he took the night off for this special occasion."

Opening his jacket, Sal proudly showed off his "GW Alumni" sweatshirt. "I totally forgot you went to GW," Mia said.

"Not just that. Football alum too," he said, holding his head high. "I was a running back in my day."

Elaine patted him on the chest. "He was pretty amazing way back when."

Mia chuckled. "Well, we're glad you could come to celebrate with us. And help yourself to a sugar-free muffin."

"Oh, thank you!" He took a plump blueberry muffin, savoring the first bite. "Wow. These are so much better than the coffee shop down the street." Mia beamed while walking away.

Within minutes, the room was overflowing with loud, excited fans of blue and gold. "Hey, Prez DeSalvo!" Abbie shouted, still clutching her crinkly pompoms and towing along her fellow cheerleaders. "Awesome speech at the game!"

Mia paused from setting out stacks of blue plastic cups on the punch table. "Thanks. It wasn't hard with such great causes behind us."

Abbie scanned the room. "Zach looked pretty great today, right?"

"Um, yeah. Sure, I guess."

Twirling her curly blonde ponytail between her fingers, she flashed a sweet smile. "Well, if you happen to see him around, tell him to stop by for a chat. Okay, Mia?"

"Uh, sure, Abbie. Will do," she said with a thumbs-up. As the cheerleader ran off, her sparkly blue and gold bow bouncing around on the tip-top of her head, Mia couldn't help but give her own head a shake.

Rushing in next with a *jingle* was Chloe, Seth timidly trailing behind—sans apron. "Hey, Mia! Missed you on the field, but sorry we're a bit late. Had to take a detour. By the way, don't expect the guys any time soon. As we were leaving, they brought out the orange and red Gatorade and totally doused everyone, even Bryce. I bet those uniforms are toast. They gotta reek like fruit cocktail."

Mia gave her long monologue a shrug. "Sorry. I had to set up here." Thrusting her chin toward Seth, she muttered, "Was *that* the detour?"

"Yeah. I had to rescue him from his parents. He'd been serving coffee since six this morning!"

Offering Seth a tight smile, Mia said flatly, "Hi. Never seen you without that green apron." Then, catching Chloe's frown, she halfheartedly extended her hand. "Fine. Officially nice to meet you."

He grinned broadly, eagerly shaking it. "Thanks. Um, listen, I know we're supposed to be kinda ..."

"Enemies?" she said, crossing her arms.

Seth's smile faded as he stepped back slightly. "I was gonna say *competitors*. But your word works too, I guess," he said, looking uncomfortable. "I thought I could present you with a peace offering." He handed Mia a cardboard box in a shocking shade of pink, with "**The hOle Deal**" printed on top in large, obnoxious purple bubble letters.

"What's this?" she asked, peeking inside. "Doughnuts?"

"Ooh. Let me see!" Chloe ripped open the top, taking out a white powdery masterpiece, dripping deep red jelly. Enjoying a large gooey bite, she muttered, "Yum. Raspberry is my favorite," shooting powdered sugar everywhere.

Mia reread the box. "What's **The hOle Deal**?"

Seth gave Chloe an unsure look. "Um. The new place down the street. I thought you knew about it."

One glance at Mia and Chloe slammed the box shut, pushing it back toward Seth. "Um, never mind. Mia has better things to worry about."

"Wait," Mia said, a cunning look in her eyes. "Let me see that box, Seth." As he handed it back to her, she added, "Thanks," with a sly smile.

"Um, Mia. Is there anything else I can do to, you know, smooth things over?"

Chloe looked hopeful as Mia mulled it over. Suddenly, her dad appeared, smartly attired in a blue dress shirt and dark slacks. "Actually, Seth. There *is* something. You're an expert at making chai lattes, right?" When he vigorously nodded, she pushed him in the direction of her dad and the espresso machine.

Once he'd walked off, Chloe squealed, "So. I have terrific news! This edition of the literary magazine has officially sold out. Our first time ever! Can you believe it?"

Mia diverted her eyes from the doughnut box. "Of course, Chloe. Especially with your editorial skills and Bryce's fantastic submission."

"I know, right? Everyone wanted to read the mind-blowing piece by our star quarterback." Leaning in, she whispered, "What'd you think of the dedication?"

"Huh? What dedication?"

"Wait. You didn't see it? Mia, didn't you turn the page?"

"Um, no," she admitted sheepishly. "What did it say?"

Chloe giggled, shaking her head. "No way! It's something you need to read for yourself, in his own words. Definitely check it out, though, to get the whole picture."

Chapter 50

Mia was groaning to herself when she trudged back into the kitchen. She dropped the doughnut box onto the counter with a grimace, sticking her tongue out, then focused her attention on filling another tray with biscotti. But no matter how hard she tried, she couldn't get Chloe's words out of her head.

Her curiosity intensified when her eyes landed on the shiny blue book. "Oh, good grief," she said, throwing her hands up. Relenting, she reached for the book and collapsed onto a stool. "Turn the page," she grumbled with a mental head slap. "Why don't I ever just turn the page?"

Drawing in a calming breath, she found the end of Bryce's piece and turned the page over as Chloe had instructed. Sure enough, there it was:

Dedicated to a very special friend, who reminded me to always remember the happy times.

Mia cut her eyes to the corner of the room and the football sitting happily on the shelf. She sucked in some air, feeling her throat tighten. Leave it to Bryce to always write something in the most beautiful yet simple way. She hugged the book to her chest, then placed it beside the football on the shelf. "Thanks for the reminder, Chloe," she muttered, grateful she didn't miss the opportunity to read something so lovely in Bryce's own words. "The whole picture," Mia repeated. Then, she remembered.

A quick peek out the kitchen door revealed the party in full swing as blue and gold kept pouring into the bakery. Sneaking around the corner, she slowly ascended the creaky steps and pushed past the old wooden door to her apartment. She tiptoed into her room and flipped the light on her nightstand.

This time, without reservation, Mia slipped her hand under her pillows and pulled out the composition book. She opened it with quivering hands, thumbing through pages of Bryce's elegant penmanship. Her stomach clenched, finding the familiar words she dreaded the most. Even now, the entry made her cringe:

> At first glance, there is a look of disdain in her eyes. But isn't it the other way around? Is this really their "top student?" Definitely NOT what you'd see at Wellington. In fact, she's a disaster, an absolute mess. But for now, I'll humor them and her.

Mia's heart ached, rereading Bryce's brutally honest words. To know, and be reminded, this was his first impression of her was difficult, to say the least. But Bryce wanted her to see the "whole picture." Didn't she owe him that, after everything?

Pushing out a sigh, she attempted to turn the page but again chickened out, slamming the book shut. Mia internally scolded herself for being a coward. "I'm brave," she whispered, hoping she believed it. With another deep breath, she opened the book and found the entry yet again. As her fingers grasped the page, she shut her eyes before turning it. When she reopened them, the words stared back at her:

> *But somehow, I am drawn to her. There is a strength and a kindness in her eyes. Like she could be your best friend and your toughest critic at the same time. I am intrigued to get to know her. Despite all my first impressions, I have this strange feeling she is very, very special.*

When Mia closed Bryce's journal for the final time, she was stunned and breathless, trying to absorb its beautiful language. She had tried so hard to hide the "real Mia," and yet he somehow knew her all along.

Shaking from head to toe, Mia rose from her bed. She dashed across the apartment and barreled down the steps, her ponytail soaring in the wake of her own breeze. Rounding the corner, she slammed head-on into Bryce's green puffer jacket. "Hey, Mia. I was looking for you, but I guess you found me first." His grin stretched wide to a full-on laugh as he steadied her shoulders. "Good tackle. You making up for lost time?"

Mia tried to catch her breath, scrambling to her feet. Their eyes locked for a long stretch of silence until she finally broke it. "Bryce, I really need to talk to you."

"Sure," he said cheerfully, following her into the kitchen. When Mia turned to face him, his dimples evaporated at what she held tightly in her hands.

Chapter 51

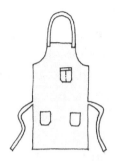

Snuggling the journal close to her chest, Mia's deep blue eyes met Bryce's uneasy hazel gaze. "Congratulations, Mr. MVP," she teased. "I heard the field got pretty crazy after I left. Guess they finally caught you."

"Yeah. Probably good you weren't there for that. Would've been impossible to get the Gatorade out of your hair." He gently tugged on some flyaway wisps from her ponytail. "I think Zach is still scrubbing it off."

"Speaking of Zach. What you did, for him and his family. Bryce, that was amazing."

"What do you mean?" he asked casually, his head lowered.

"The donation." Bryce looked up with his eyes as bright as silver dollars. "Yeah. Harper told me. Mind if I ask how you got your dad to do it?"

"I decided not to underestimate him, like you said. And I kinda showed him something I wrote ..."

"The literary magazine, right?" she asked, and he nodded. "Bryce, your piece was incredible. Your mom would've loved it."

"You think?"

"No doubt. And Chloe told me they've sold out, so I guess everyone else loved it, too."

Bryce fiddled with his jacket's zipper. "Well, I'm just glad *you* liked it. It was your idea, Mia. All of it."

Silence fell between them while she gathered more courage. "Is that also why you're not going back to Wellington?"

"Yeah. I finally told my dad what this place has meant." He fixed his gaze on Mia. As he stepped closer, her cheeks burned. "I sat down and talked to him during dinner. Can you believe it? *He* made dinner." Bryce shook his head and chuckled.

"Wow. I guess I underestimated him, too." Mia joined his laughter before her tone grew more serious. "I saw the Wellington guy at the game. I thought you were going to announce you were going back." She aimlessly toed the tile floor with her sneaker.

"Nope. Coach Miller and I were pretty close at Wellington. He was really there for me when... Anyway, he gave me some exciting news. Looks like Sebastian is coming back to Wellington next fall. And they're gonna try him out as quarterback."

"That's awesome, Bryce."

"I'm just glad things are better for him at home."

Following his gaze back to the composition book, Mia untucked it from her arms. "I need to give this back to you."

"I guess you read it, then."

"Yes," she said softly.

He accepted the journal and shuffled it back and forth in his shaky hands. "So?"

Trying to maintain eye contact, Mia inched closer to Bryce, the toes of their sneakers touching. As she held his gaze, his eyes seemed to search hers. Giving him her most stern look, she slowly punched him in the arm. "You're something else, Bryce Fitzgerald," she said, a mischievous grin forming on her face.

His adorable dimples emerged, making her heart flutter. "Oh, really?"

She nodded, staring deeply into his hazel eyes, now reflecting the green of his puffer jacket and the blue in her apron. As Mia's balanced on her tiptoes, her pulse started to race. She drew in an unsteady breath and hesitated, wondering if her next move was the right one. "And you're an amazing writer," she whispered, brushing her warm lips against his. When she backed away, Bryce's cheeks matched the exact shade of the Wellington crest.

"Thanks," he said with a coy grin. "Actually, that reminds me." He unzipped his jacket and handed Mia something wrapped in several sheets of tissue paper.

Intrigued, she started carefully removing the paper. When she'd unwrapped the last of it, Mia gasped at a dark blue cloth book sitting in her hands. She ran her fingertips over the flowery fabric, pausing in the center where it formed an ornate letter "M." "Bryce, this is beautiful."

"You said you wanted to start writing. So, I thought this might work as a journal. Or ..." he started, pointing to the corner shelf. "Maybe you could jot down some of your own recipes. In case someone in the future wanted to risk their neck for a chocolate cornetto or a gluten-free brownie," he teased.

"I could only wish." She reached up and embraced him tightly. "Thank you, Bryce."

Pulling away, he looked down at the abandoned half-filled tray of biscotti. "Need any help?"

"Actually. I'm glad you asked." Mia shot him a sly look and slid the Pepto Bismol-colored box toward him.

"What's this?"

"Our next 'good offense.'"

With curious eyes, he opened the bubble-gum pink box. "Doughnuts?"

"Yup. And I'm thinking we can get some ideas from my amazing Nonna Antoinette. You game?"

"Absolutely!" Bryce lifted a snowy doughnut from the box and took a large bite, launching fluffy white particles in every direction.

Mia giggled, brushing powdered sugar off his formerly pristine puffer coat. "Geez, Bryce. Look at you! You're an absolute mess!"

Glossary of Italian Terms

Biscotti (plural form of **Biscotto**) – A crisp cookie that is twice-baked

Buon giorno or **Buongiorno** – "Good morning"

Cannoli (plural form of **Cannolo**) – A Sicilian pastry consisting of a fried tube-shaped shell filled with a sweet, creamy filling, usually made with a ricotta base and sprinkled with a topping of pistachios or chocolate chips

Cornetti (plural form of **Cornetto**) – Meaning "little horn;" a pastry similar to a croissant, but softer and containing less butter

Fiori di Sicilia – Meaning "flowers of Sicily," a highly-concentrated extract used in baking that contains essences of floral, citrus, and vanilla

Grazie – "You are welcome"

Nonna – "Grandmother"

Panettone – A Christmas cake originating in Milan; sweet, domeshaped, usually containing candied fruits and nuts

Pandoro – A Christmas cake originating in Verona; star-shaped and dusted with powdered sugar; meaning "golden bread," it is bright yellow in color

Papà – Affectionate name for "Dad," "Daddy," or "Pa"

Author's Note

An author only gets one debut novel, so I sincerely thank you for supporting mine to these very last pages. The idea for Mia and her GW High pals originated after one of my holiday baking sessions. As someone who finds great joy in bringing new life into my family's old recipes, I couldn't resist writing a story about keeping those treasured memories alive.

A few fun tidbits about the novel:

Fiora di Sicilia, a.k.a. "Flower of Sicily Extract," is an actual special ingredient in Italian baking.

A *Flea Flicker* is a real "trick play" in American football.

Initially, I hadn't intended for football to play such a huge role in the story. But my love for sports is so deeply ingrained, it somehow always weaves its way into my writing.

Bryce's number 5 jersey, first worn by Captain Redding, was inspired by Syracuse University quarterbacks

Donovan McNabb and Eric Dungey (now number 5 for the Cincinnati Bengals). For Zach's number, I included my alma mater's legendary Syracuse #44, made famous by running backs: Jim Brown, Ernie Davis, and Floyd Little.

Mia's baking mentor and great-great-grandmother was inspired by the real Antoinette DeSalvo, my husband's great-grandmother, who emigrated from Sicily in the early 1900's.

The Real Antoinette DeSalvo

Antonietta "Antoinette" DeSalvo (1890-1980) with her husband Bernardo "Bernard" Perdichizzi (1878-1963) On the day of their wedding (July 7, 1911), Manhattan, New York City, New York

Acknowledgments

Despite my author credit on the cover, no writer is ever alone along the long road to publication. My story of unwavering friendship, through loss and triumph, came to life on the printed page because of the support and encouragement of many who saw something special in Mia and her journey. A sincere thank you . . .

To my awesome first beta reader, Maggie. This story and genre couldn't be more different from your own writing, but you still managed to fall in love with Mia and her friends more and more with each turn of the digital page. Your enthusiasm reminded this debut author how special her story was and how important it was to share it.

To my author-mentors, Brandy and Leyna, whose invaluable advice and encouragement kept me going through all the bumps in the road.

To my editor, Sarah, who probably learned more about apostrophe usage in sports writing than she ever wanted to know.

To Cheryl, for graciously reading my stories for both enjoyment and correct comma placement.

To Lane, for your eagle eye proofreading skills and appreciation for Italian baking and culture. I owe you some cannoli, overflowing with pistachios!

To that elderly stranger in Stockbridge, who overheard a few words of a conversation and wished me luck on my book, reminding me that—yes—this is a big deal.

To the "Original 7," for your support through one heck of a ride. I still think one of us should pen the story. Write on, ladies!

To my supremely talented, dream cover designer Michael, for bringing vibrant and colorful life to Mia and Bryce. I could think of no other illustrator who could capture this sport's story in such an authentic way.

To my family. Much love and thank you for raising me to be as strong-willed as Mia, and letting me test it, frequently.

To Jonathan, for too much to put down on paper. I'm sure your proudest contribution to this project is that you invented the "Urban Uber." I kind of don't blame you.

And finally, a most sincere thank you to my young readers. I hope Mia's journey inspires you to become your own hero in everyday life.

About The Author

Kelly Swan Taylor is a Boston-based attorney and former laboratory scientist. As a competitive runner, racing from sun-drenched Hawaii to frigid Iceland, her first publishing credit was in Simon & Schuster's best-selling book series, *Chicken Soup for the Soul, Running for Good*, highlighting her experiences in the historic 2013 and 2014 Boston Marathons. Growing up immersed in beloved "Teen" novels, Kelly now crafts her own sweet stories that bridge the gap between middle grade and young adult fiction that is so often forgotten but so sorely needed in the market today. She has a soft spot for the sincere yet flawed character with a kind heart who tries to do the right thing, stumbles along the way, but eventually becomes a hero in everyday life. In her free time, Kelly enjoys traveling and collecting snow globes and race medals from around the world. A proud alumnus of Syracuse University, she cheers her Syracuse Orange from both her sofa and the metal bleachers of the Carrier Dome. She resides in Providence, Rhode Island with her architect husband, Jonathan, and two spoiled geriatric kitties, Otto & Kona.

You can connect with Kelly on various social media
platforms and subscribe to her newsletter
via linktr.ee/KellySwanTaylor.

Coming Spring 2022 from this author:
The Wright Detective Series

Celebrate with Mia and her
George Washington Eagles football team
with patriotic gear from 1776United.com

15% sitewide promo code: *WinningIngredient*

About Link Press

*The goal of Link Press is to bridge the gap
between middle grade and young adult fiction that
is so necessary in the marketplace but so often forgotten.*

With the aging up of young adult fiction over the past couple of decades, teen readers are increasingly being left out. Parents, teachers, librarians, and especially readers walk into bookstores and find they are wedged between two sections that are often too young or too old. To complicate matters, young readers tend to "read up." So, to the shock of parents, their 12-year-olds are stuck reading very adult stories with 17-year-old protagonists. Anyone can tell you, life is very different from the ages of 12 to 17.

Therefore, writers need to bridge that gap. But the publishing industry is just as confused as the readers. What do you do with a 13 or 14-year-old protagonist? Sadly, the current answer is nothing. Publishers are reluctant to print those stories. The simple suggestion is to change the age of the protagonist. The result is that the formative, all-important years between middle school and high school are obliterated in fiction just because an age range doesn't fit into a mold.

While writers of children's literature should always be encouraged to pen the stories that move them, tweens and teens should be part of that movement. At Link Press, young readers are always the primary focus.

As an author with this innovative press, Kelly Swan Taylor is passionate about filling that middle grade-young adult gap and bringing these stories back to the readers. Link Press believes there is an indelible connection between these reading age groups that forms a strong bond for strong storytelling.

Want to learn more about Link Press?

Visit authorklswantaylor.wixsite.com/home/link-press.

Mia's Almond/Pistachio Biscotti

Ingredients:
(all at room temperature)
- 1 cup whole almonds/pistachios raw
- 2-1/4 cups all-purpose flour
- 1 1/2 teaspoons baking powder
- 1/2 teaspoon salt
- 1/2 cup granulated sugar
- 3/4 cup brown sugar
- 3 large eggs
- 6 tablespoons of olive oil
- 2 tablespoons of unsalted butter
- 1 teaspoon pure vanilla extract or
- 1/2 teaspoon of pure vanilla extract and 1/2 teaspoon of almond extract
- 1 teaspoon lemon zest

Instructions:
Preheat oven to 325° F.

Position rack in center of oven.

Coarsely chop nuts (almonds or pistachios), then spread evenly on a baking sheet.

Toast in oven for 12–15 minutes.

Meanwhile, blend dry ingredients in a bowl with a whisk and set aside.

In a stand mixer with a paddle attachment, combine butter and sugars. Add eggs, olive oil, extracts, and zest. Mix lightly together.

When nuts are toasted, remove from oven.

Line sheet pan with parchment paper or a baking mat.

Add dry ingredients to wet mixture, then cooled almonds/pistachios, mixing until just incorporated.

Using damp hands or a nonstick spoon, scoop out the dough (it will be sticky) and place it on a sheet pan, dividing it into two equal logs (about 14 inches long, 2-1/2 inches wide); keep in mind, these will puff up and spread in the oven.

Bake for approximately 30 minutes or until edges are lightly brown in color and firm. Allow to cool for about 10 minutes (don't wait too long because the dough will crumble when cutting).

Remove from baking sheet and transfer to cutting board.

Using a serrated knife, slice cookies at an angle about 1/2–3/4 inches thick.

Lay slices flat on the baking sheet and bake for another 15–20 minutes or up to desired crispiness. Turn them over at the halfway mark.

Place on a wire rack to cool.

Enjoy with your favorite coffee or cappuccino.